"I want to know the *real* reason I'm here on your ranch."

"You know what they say about curiosity," Zack said blandly.

"And you know what they say about wolves and sheep's clothing," Alex returned. "All right. You've had your fun. And now I'm here alone, completely at your mercy—which is what you wanted."

He shrugged.

"Please have the decency to tell me *why* you've gone to these elaborate lengths," she went on. "Neither my brother nor I had ever seen you in our lives—not until you walked through our shop door that day. If we've done something to offend you, just tell me, and we'll apologize!"

Zack stared hard at her. "I make it a policy never to discuss business until my guest is comfortable," he murmured. "Since you'll be spending the night at the Circle Q, I suggest we retire to the house. We'll talk...later."

Dear Reader,

I'm delighted, once again, to be included in one of Harlequin Romance's special collections. I'm especially delighted that it's the Back to the Ranch series.

To me, the word *ranch* is practically synonymous with "romance." When I was a youngster, my favorite television show was set in the West; it was called "Sky King" after its hero. This handsome, larger-than-life rancher and his niece, Penny, lived on a spread so large he had to fly his own plane in order to inspect it from one end to the other. Every woman who visited his ranch fell in love with Sky King, and so did I!

He was the epitome of the perfect male—a ruggedly handsome individualist, a protector of women and children, a lover of animals and nature, self-sufficient. He loved his family, the land, the country. He was irresistible to women.

In my story, *The Rancher and the Redhead,* I've tried to create my own Sky King in the form of Zackery Quinn, a Nevada rancher who owns and runs the renowned Circle Q. He's a modern cowboy who possesses all those wonderful, romantic Old West qualities.

In fact, I've enjoyed writing Zack Quinn's story so much, I'm already thinking about a book featuring his brother-in-law, another Nevada-born-and-bred hero.

Because there's nothing like those Western men....

Sincerely,

Rebecca Winters

THE RANCHER AND THE REDHEAD
Rebecca Winters

Harlequin Books

TORONTO • NEW YORK • LONDON
AMSTERDAM • PARIS • SYDNEY • HAMBURG
STOCKHOLM • ATHENS • TOKYO • MILAN
MADRID • WARSAW • BUDAPEST • AUCKLAND

To Rosalie White, WA1STO,
Educational Activities Manager at
The American Radio Relay League (ARRL),
for her invaluable help in showing me the joys of
ham radio.

To Deborah, whose contributions about ranch life
made all the difference.

ISBN 0-373-03280-3

Harlequin Romance first edition September 1993

THE RANCHER AND THE REDHEAD

CHAPTER ONE

"N6HUT, THIS IS N6AFW," Randy Cordell called over the ham radio set while he stuffed a copy of the American Radio Relay League's latest magazine into his suitcase. "I repeat, this is N6AFW." He glanced out his bedroom window at the driveway and breathed a sigh of relief; his Uncle Zack hadn't arrived yet.

Randy had hoped to make contact with Troy before leaving Carson City for his uncle's ranch. He didn't dare use the phone in case someone listened in on one of a dozen other extensions. That was a major drawback of living in the governor's mansion—his father's staff was always checking up on him.

"This is N6HUT," Troy answered. "Go ahead, Jerry."

Jerry Spaulding was the fake name Randy used over ham radio to protect his father's name. In fact he'd made up a fake family so Troy could never guess his real identity. "I'm afraid I've got some news that's going to complicate our plans a little. You'll have to get in touch with Steve right away."

"What's wrong? Please don't tell me you got caught—not when business is booming!"

"No way. Listen, how long can we talk? Is your sister around? This is important, Troy."

"Alex went to the grocery store, but she'll be back in a few minutes, so hurry up and tell me what's going on. If she ever finds out what we're doing, she'll kill us. She doesn't have red hair for nothing!"

"Okay. Here's the story. My, uh, parents are leaving on a family vacation and I don't want to go. Problem is, they won't let me live at Steve's while they're gone, so I have to stay with relatives."

"Don't like the idea, huh?"

"You got that right!"

"How long will they be gone?"

"I don't know. A couple of weeks. Maybe longer."

"That'll put us behind schedule."

"I know, and my relatives don't have a ham set. But I can help Steve with the mailings if you guys'll send me the stuff."

"Why can't you just stay home by yourself? Think of the contacts you could make over the radio while they're gone!"

"Try telling my dad that. He thinks I'll raise hell while he's . . . while they're away. I heard him talking to my relatives. He told them to watch me like a hawk and work me so hard I'll be too tired to get into any trouble. I don't want to get on their bad side, so I'm going to have to be careful. We'll only be able to talk on the phone when nobody's around, and that won't be easy. You and Steve are going to have to be ready for my calls when they come."

"No sweat. This busted leg guarantees I'm not going anyplace. What's their address? I'll send you a shipment next week. I could do more, but I have to be careful, too—so Alex won't get suspicious."

"Yeah. Just send the box to Jerry Spaulding, in care of Yolanda Montoya, Star Route 9, off Highway 95, Yerington, Nevada. Got all that?"

"Yeah. Who's this Yolanda?"

Randy had to think fast. "Uh . . . she's the house-keeper at my relatives' place, and she's crazy about me. She'll help us out, no questions asked. How many posters do you have done?" He changed the subject as quickly as he could.

"Six dozen, and they're pure dynamite."

"That's great!" Randy said, relieved that Troy hadn't pursued the subject of Yolanda. "Make sure you send the box Express Air," he went on. "They always deliver by ten in the morning."

"Good. We've really got to keep this under wraps, Jerry."

"Hey, we've done fine so far. Did Steve tell you we got another 120 orders?"

"Yeah. Since we made up those brochures, the or-ders have tripled. Thank goodness school's out! I fig-ure that by next March we'll reach our goal of $120,000 profit. Even with the printing expenses and the costs of the mailing tubes and postage, we could each make almost $35,000. Not bad for a year's work. It means I'll be able to pay my own way through col-lege."

"Not me, man," said Randy. "I want to buy that sweet Jag. I was thinking we ought to start sending catalogues to Japan. Did you read in *Amateur Radio* that the Japanese have no-code licensing? And their ham magazines are huge compared to ours. We ought to be able to clean up there."

"You're right. You know how much they like American celebrities and stuff."

"And we've already got a break in the Scandinavian countries. I reached a guy in some place called Vastertorp, Sweden, last week. He's placed an order, and if he likes what we send him, he'll get us a whole bunch of local call signs."

"That's great. And I've been talking to some guys in Germany. They're crazy about our brochure. I made a deal with them to send us call signs by offering some freebies as incentive."

Randy grinned. "That's sweet. Yes my man, the field is white and ready to harvest."

"You can say that again."

"D'you need any cash for supplies? I can always pawn my new golf clubs."

"Nope. We've made enough money so you don't have to put up any more. Pretty soon you'll be able to buy back all the stuff you pawned when we were getting the business started."

"Well, let me know if there's a problem. Uh-oh. I think I hear a car in the driveway. Gotta run. Talk to you later. Don't forget to tell Steve. This is N6AFW signing off for now."

A HOT JUNE SUN glinted off Zackery Quinn's black hair as he left the shed and reached his half-ton pickup in a few swift strides.

One of his mechanics was still held up repairing a hay baler because a couple of parts for the knotter hadn't arrived from Carson City yet. Since Zack's field foreman urgently needed the baler, Zack decided to drive into town and get the parts himself.

While he was there he'd see if his friend Miguel could join him and Randy for lunch at the Biscay Inn, the world-famous Basque restaurant Miguel's family had owned and operated for almost a hundred years.

But even if Miguel was too involved with his work at the university to meet them in Carson City, Zack looked forward to chatting with his friend's mother. Begona Aldabe knew more about the local ranching community than virtually anyone else. And the atmosphere at the inn was conducive to a serious talk with Randy. The boy had been unusually quiet and evasive since his arrival at the ranch. He'd agreed to clean out the storeroom this morning without giving Zack an argument. That in itself made Zack want to know the reason why.

Climbing into the cab, he started the truck and headed for the main house three miles away, his lungs drawing in the sweet smell of alfalfa. It was like the breath of life to him. The day he couldn't ride the range and muster cattle with his cowhands, the day he couldn't savor the beauty of sunrise stealing over the miles of pastureland belonging to the Circle Q, was the day he didn't want to go on living.

A pain shot through Zack when he thought of his father, also named Zackery, confined to a wheelchair back at the house. After three paralyzing strokes, he couldn't even talk. But Zack figured his father could still see and hear and smell. Every morning after breakfast Zack pushed the wheelchair onto the upstairs deck so the once-vital rancher could look out over the land he loved every bit as fiercely as Zack did. At least he could relive his memories.

As the truck reached the gravel drive leading up to the front porch of the house, Zack's thoughts were diverted by a movement he caught from the corner of his eye. He discovered an Express Air van pulling away, in the direction of the highway. It occurred to Zack that maybe he wouldn't be driving to town, after all. But he and Randy were still going to have that talk, preferably sometime today.

"Yolanda? Where are you?" he called to his housekeeper a few minutes later as he walked through the foyer of the ranch house.

"I'm in the kitchen."

When Zack appeared in the doorway, she looked up from the potted plant she was soaking in the sink. "Jocco just phoned and said to call him as soon as you could." Zack nodded. "What are you doing home this time of day? You only ate breakfast a few hours ago."

He smiled at the sixty-year-old Mexican woman. Married to one of the best stockmen on the ranch, she was like family. "I was going to run into town to pick up some machine parts, but it looks like they've been delivered, so I'm saved a trip."

Yolanda shook her head. "I'm afraid that was a package for Randy."

Zack frowned. His thoughts focused on his brother-in-law, Andrew, who did a far better job as governor of the state of Nevada than he did as a father. Since the death of Zack's sister Wendie, twenty months earlier, Andrew had buried himself in work. Right now he was off on yet another political tour. "Doesn't

Andrew know Randy needs *him,* not more presents?''

"That's the way of some men," Yolanda said philosophically. "In their grief they forget those closest to them. But before you jump to conclusions, keep in mind the only thing that's come from Andrew so far is a postcard."

Yolanda had a soft spot for Randy, the only child Andrew and Wendie were able to have. The rare blood disorder that finally killed her had made further pregnancies impossible. Zack, too, had always felt a special affection for his complicated nephew, who bore a marked resemblance to Wendie. But in Zack's opinion, the boy had been given too much too soon in life; he supposed it was Andrew's way of compensating.

Randy had difficulty relating to his busy father. As a result, he'd gotten into trouble, first with drinking, then drugs. He was a constant source of worry and embarrassment to Andrew, who struggled to keep news of his son's problems from leaking to the press. "I think I'll go check on his progress and see if he wants to drive into town with me."

To Zack's surprise, the storeroom off the kitchen appeared to be pretty well emptied, and everything had been neatly stacked outside on the back porch. His nephew had made a good start, but he'd left his task unfinished.

Wondering if the package had something to do with Randy's disappearance, he quickened his pace through the hall and up the stairs to his nephew's room.

Zack hesitated only a moment before knocking on the door. "Randy? Are you in there?"

He heard the crash of a chair and a stream of swear words. "Yeah? What do you want, Uncle Zack? I thought you weren't coming back until lunch."

"I decided to see how the storeroom was coming along. Thought I'd lend a hand so we could have a talk at the same time. How about it?"

"Uh...I don't like to keep you from your work, Uncle Zack. I can finish by myself."

"I don't doubt it." Deciding this had gone far enough, he said, "Are you all right?"

"Sure."

"I heard a crash."

"My chair tipped over by accident."

"Why don't you come out on the deck and have some lemonade with me and grandpa before you and I have to get back to work?"

After a long pause he heard his nephew mutter, "Okay." The minute Randy opened his door, Zack's keen gaze took in the huge box sitting on the floor and dozens of mailing tubes piled on the bed.

"It looks like you've got a big project going there. Something for your dad?"

Randy nodded his head. "Yeah. I thought I'd help him out while he's gone." A nervous smile came and went. "Now that you mention it, a lemonade sounds good."

But Zack's tall muscled body blocked the doorway and made it impossible for Randy to step around him. "Can I see what you're doing? Maybe I can help."

"No. It's kind of a private project."

"Maybe so, but we're family. Right?" He tousled his nephew's dark hair and moved quickly into the bedroom. As he reached for a tube, Randy's face blanched.

"I'd rather you kept out of my business, Uncle Zack. I get enough of that at home."

Zack regarded his nephew shrewdly. "I'm sorry, Randy, but maybe that's because there's usually trouble attached to your business." In the next instant he tore open the seal on one end of the tube and pulled out the contents.

Wondering what he'd uncover, he unrolled a fourteen-by-twenty-inch full-color poster and found himself staring at the picture of a barefoot woman washing a compact car with a sponge. She wore cutoffs and a T-shirt. And while there was nothing indecent about the picture, her gorgeous legs seemed to go on forever, and her well-endowed body radiated a sensuality he'd rarely seen in any woman.

His gaze moved to the classic oval shape of her face with its flawless skin, then to the cascade of glossy red-gold hair tied back with a narrow black ribbon. Beneath those provocative curls and laughing dark blue eyes, a wide full mouth smiled out at him, hinting of innocent and temptress all at once. Across the bottom was written, "To Mark, Love Alexandria."

Only an expert photographer and a model who knew exactly what to do in front of the camera could come up with a picture that looked so natural and unposed. To his dismay, Zack found himself attracted to the beautiful woman on display. He couldn't account for it, especially since calendar pinups hadn't appealed to him since his early university days.

When he thought back thirteen years, he recalled that the casinos and strip shows in Tahoe and Reno had held a certain fascination for him and his college buddies. Until he'd fallen for a showgirl who wanted much more out of life than marriage to what she assumed was a struggling college student. She wasn't about to be saddled with an out-of-work husband and a bunch of screaming kids, she'd bluntly told him.

Her rejection had hurt like hell, and despite his family's pleadings, Zack had left home to travel through Europe with Miguel. Meeting other women took away some of the pain until he returned home and learned a few things from Andrew, who by then had joined a law firm and had his own sources of information. The woman Zack had once asked to be his wife acted in porno films when she wasn't performing in sleazy stage shows.

To make matters uglier, while Zack was in Europe someone had told her he was a Quinn of the Circle Q, and she'd tried to extort money from his wealthy father by threatening to expose her relationship with Zack to the media.

Zack's father had quickly squelched her blackmailing scheme. He told the woman she'd had her chance to inherit millions when Zack proposed to her, and if she didn't get out of their lives, he'd hire an attorney to make sure she stayed away. The threat worked, and she'd left the Reno area for good.

Since the day Andrew had told him all this, Zack's love for his father had increased a hundredfold. The older man had never once blamed him for his poor judgment, nor had he ever brought up the incident again. Needless to say, any lingering yearnings for the woman he had wanted to marry had turned into feelings of revulsion....

A scowl marred his features. The experience had permanently altered his perception of women who performed on or off camera.

"She's a fine-looking woman, isn't she?" Randy said in a tone of forced enthusiasm.

Zack ignored his nephew, put the poster on the bed and opened another tube. The same captivating woman stared back at him, but this time she wore a long-sleeved tailored blouse tucked in at the waist of her jeans while she washed dishes at a kitchen sink. Her hair bounced around her shoulders and she was looking at the camera as if surprised. The curves of her luscious figure were in full evidence because of the way the sun shone through the window. This one was inscribed, "To Rex, Love, Alexandria."

Zack could feel the chemistry. Almost against his will he reached for one more tube and opened it. This time he saw her in a close-up shot, wearing what appeared to be a bathrobe.

She was brushing her hair, and her dark blue eyes held a faraway expression, as if she was deep in thought. She looked as sexy as hell, and seemingly unaware that a camera had captured this private side of her. The inscription read, "To Ryan, Love, Alexandria."

He threw the poster on the bed and turned to his nephew. "Do you want to tell me what this is all about? And I don't want to hear how this is going to help your dad with his next political campaign."

AN HOUR LATER Zack headed for his study, any thoughts of driving to town forgotten. He flipped open his private telephone directory and punched in a number he found on the first page. Bud Atkins, a private investigator and longtime friend of the family, had helped in previous delicate situations involving Randy.

He chatted with Bud's secretary for a minute and then Bud himself came on the line. "Zack, you son of a gun! How're you doing? Haven't seen you around for a while."

"The ranch takes all my time, you know that, Bud." He paced back and forth behind his desk. "How come you haven't been out fishing? You're always welcome."

"I'd love it, but I'm up to my neck in work. How's your dad? And Randy? I heard he was staying with you. That was one of Andrew's better ideas."

Zack grimaced, pausing in midstride. "Bud—Randy's in trouble. Again."

"How bad?"

"I don't know. That's what I've got to find out. Do me a favor, will you? And not a word of this to Andrew. If I can put a lid on it, he'll never have to know."

"My lips are sealed. So, what've you got?"

"I need you to find out everything you can about the people running a typesetting shop for camera-ready ads in Reno. I don't have an address but it's called the Write Set-Up. And Bud, I mean *everything.*"

"In that case, it'll probably take me until tomorrow night."

"Good. Call me, no matter how late."

"Will do. Talk to you later."

As soon as they hung up, Zack called Jocco, who filled him in on a problem with some of the cattle. It meant that immediate action was necessary, and the rest of Zack's day would be spent on the range. He'd have to forgo calling Miguel until evening. His friend always kept a cool head, and Zack wanted to discuss Randy with him, but that would have to wait.

Before Zack left the house, he took a detour to his father's room, nodding to the nurse, Noreen, who was putting clean sheets on the bed.

His father was still in the wheelchair on the veranda, where Zack had left him earlier, his head drooped over his chest, eyes closed. As he observed his father's helplessness, Zack felt a familiar tightening in his throat.

Getting down on his haunches, he reached for the frail hand of the once-hardy rancher and laid it against his cheek. "Dad? I'm afraid I'm going to have to be gone all day. Jocco discovered some sick cattle out in the south pasture, and I need to inspect the other herds to see if it's an isolated problem or not. My hunch is something has contaminated the water from that one hole. What do you think?"

After half a minute or so Zack felt his father's thumb press ever so slightly against his fingers. He wanted to believe his father was still trying to communicate with him.

"Good. I'm glad you agree. As soon as Randy finishes his job in the storeroom, he's going to keep you company." Zack's voice thickened with emotion. "He loves you, Dad. So do I," he murmured. "Thank God you're here for us."

Zack got to his feet, gave his father a kiss on the forehead and left for the south pasture.

By the end of the next day, after a thorough inspection of the herds, Zack's theory had proven correct. The saline level in the one watering hole was too high. Zack gave orders to fence it off and move the rest of the cattle to the adjacent pasture as a temporary measure. The hole could be drying up; only time would tell.

Late that night, after a long shower to wash away the grime of a grueling day beneath a scorching sun, Zack was at his desk, catching up on correspondence, when the phone rang. "Circle Q," he answered automatically.

"Hi. It's Bud. You said to call no matter how late, so I took you at your word."

"I was hoping it was you. Go ahead."

"Before I tell you what I found, I'm curious to know what it was that first made you suspicious."

Zack's brow furrowed. "In the past few months it seems Randy's gotten himself involved in a shady mail-order scheme selling posters of a gorgeous redhead. There seem to be three of them on the selling end—all teenage boys—and the pictures are apparently of the one boy's sister. They've raked in more than $20,000 already, using ham radio to make contacts with other ham buffs clear from Reno to Germany.

"Randy hasn't got a clue if they have a business license or pay any income tax. Considering all the trouble he's been in, Randy is still so damn naive! He's never even met any of the people involved or signed a contract. All the soliciting has been done over the air, which goes against ARRL regulations. He managed to get a post-office box so that the other two characters—the kid called Troy and his sister—can send Randy and his friend Steven their share of the cash. In the beginning my nephew pawned a lot of his personal things, like his stereo, his VCR and a couple of cameras, to help provide the funds."

Bud whistled.

"Naturally I've told Randy that apart from everything else, he's underage and needs to get out of this immediately. But until I know the bottom line, we'll have to proceed with extreme caution."

Bud released a long sigh. "What you've just told me makes what I've discovered that much more fascinating. The woman whose name appears on the business license of the Write Set-Up comes out so squeaky clean, someone ought to erect a monument to her. I knew she sounded too good to be true. Now it's starting to make sense."

Zack picked up a pen to take notes. "Go on," he urged.

"Okay. For starters, the woman's name is Alexandria Fitzroy Duncan. She's twenty-four, never been married, was born and raised in Grass Valley, California. She has an impressive secondary-school record. Hope of America award from Kiwanis, National Merit Scholar in English, member of high school choir that traveled to Europe, editor of the yearbook staff, nominated as governor of Girls' State in Sacramento her senior year.

"Her parents were well-thought-of by their neighbors and ran a modest photography studio until their death three years ago. They were killed in a train crash, leaving her and the younger brother you mentioned—Troy—the only survivors. At that time she'd been enrolled for two years as an undergraduate on scholarship at the University of Nevada, with a cumulative grade-point average of 3.8. She was supporting herself by working at a pancake house where she received glowing accolades from the manager, who remembered her.

"After the death of her parents, she dropped out of college, and with her brother's help kept the studio going, expanding it to a legitimate photo and typesetting business. The license is up-to-date and she's paid her income tax every year, on time.

"Last fall, her brother, who was some kind of local football hero, received a serious injury and underwent several operations. He had to go on home study. Three months ago she sold the family home in Grass Valley and moved to Reno, where she bought a house. Relocated the business, called it the Write Set-Up.

"Neither she nor her brother has ever had a brush with the law. No speeding tickets, no drinking, no drugs. Never filed for bankruptcy. She holds a U.S. passport and was a registered voter in California. She owes no outstanding bills, uses one credit card, and they drive an '85 Honda. I have no information about the men in her life.''

Zack lunged to his feet, his features grim. ''We couldn't possibly be talking about the same woman, Bud.'' He grabbed a poster from the box he'd taken out of Randy's room, the one showing her outside washing the car. ''I have the proof in my hands.''

''I hear you, Zack. And I agree there's something fishy about anyone that perfect.''

Perfect wasn't the word, Zack muttered to himself, unable to prevent his eyes from studying her dimensions and those long shapely legs one more time.

''Zack?''

''I'm here, Bud.''

''What do you want me to do now?''

''Nothing more for the moment. Something tells me *she's* the brains behind this little family business. She's obviously been manipulating this younger brother of hers.'' His voice tightened with contempt. ''I've got a plan to find out if I'm right and I'll let you know if I need anything else. You've helped more than you know, Bud. Andrew and I both thank you. Expect a bonus in the mail.''

''TROY? WHAT ARE YOU doing in there? Get off the radio and come to breakfast, please.''

''Okay. I'm coming.'' His face lit up when he saw the scones Alex carried to the table. ''Hey, those are my favorite. What's the occasion?'' He rested his crutches against another chair and sat down, stretching out his leg in its heavy cast.

"Since it's the first day of summer vacation and your homeroom teacher told me you did so well on your finals, I thought we'd celebrate."

"Thanks, Alex." When they were both seated at the table, she smiled at her sandy-haired brother. Troy had to be lonely for friends since their recent move from California, and he probably felt like a prisoner after so much physical inactivity. "Did I tell you that Ron Sealey called the other day?"

Troy paused before biting into another honey-laden scone. "You mean the guy who owns the auto-parts shop? The one who has the hots for you?"

She frowned. "Yes, and I wish you wouldn't use that expression. I did an ad for him. Anyway, he said he might be able to use you in the back room of his store, looking up supplies on the computer and ordering more stock. He told me to bring you in today and he'd have a talk with you."

"Today?" he exploded, his mouth full of scone.

"Troy, what's wrong?"

He chewed rapidly and swallowed, shaking his head. "Look, Alex, it's not that I don't appreciate it, but that's the last place I'd want to work. Now that I can get around on crutches, I'd prefer finding my own job. As a matter of fact, I'm working on a couple of projects right now. Can't you tell him I've already found something else? Besides, you need me to do the photography when you're busy with the ads."

The food suddenly lost its flavor, and Alex put down her fork. "You know jobs for kids your age are hard to come by, Troy—especially for a boy in your condition. What if nothing else works out? You need to keep busy this summer. I appreciate your helping me when I need expert photography done, but those jobs don't pop up all that often, and they don't give you any spending money."

"I'm working on some ideas," he muttered. "Just give me time and I'll start making a lot more than five bucks an hour."

She couldn't help admiring his confidence, but to say she had reservations about his chances was putting it mildly. "Most seventeen-year-olds would be happy with that wage."

"Don't worry," he muttered, swallowing another bite of scone. "I'll be eighteen in a couple of months. And this stupid cast'll come off soon. Then I won't be a burden to you anymore." On a burst of emotion, he shoved himself away from the table and limped from the kitchen. Alex heard his bedroom door slam.

Her first impulse was to go after him and make peace, but the front buzzer was ringing, indicating her first client of the day. She hurried to the front of the house, which she'd converted to a storefront and studio-cum-darkroom.

Alex recognized the woman immediately. Shannon Gordon was a local artist of growing repute; her watercolors were gaining her a national following. There'd been several articles about her in local papers and magazines recently, and Alex had seen her work in a nearby gallery. That was where they'd met.

Pleased that Shannon apparently remembered their meeting, Alex greeted her with a wide smile. "I'm thrilled to see you again. And I have to tell you that if

I had the money, I'd buy your latest painting, that one of the Mission in Santa Barbara.''

The other woman beamed with pleasure. ''Thank you. It's one of my favorites, too. In fact, I've decided to advertise a series on the early missions of the West—which is why I'm here. I mentioned you to a friend who works for the library, and she said you did a wonderful job on a flyer for them last month. I need some flyers made up and wondered if you'd help me with the ad.''

''I'd be honored. Let me see what you have in mind.''

Together the two of them pored over the woman's sketch. Alex made a few suggestions, showed her several examples of typeface and quoted a price for everything, including the color transparency, which the other woman found more than reasonable.

''Come by tomorrow after three, and I'll have it ready for the printers.''

''So soon?'' Shannon exclaimed. ''That's wonderful! I want to get them printed as quickly as possible so I can take them around to the different galleries.''

''Bring some of your flyers here,'' Alex suggested. ''I'll hand them out to any customers I think might be interested.''

''You're an angel. Thanks.''

As the woman turned to leave, another person entered the shop. Business seemed awfully brisk for only nine-fifteen in the morning. Alex hoped it would keep up like this the rest of the summer so she could save some money for Troy's college. She wasn't going to let anything prevent her brother from getting his education. She frowned slightly, wondering why he was so moody and difficult these days.

Glancing up from the counter to greet her new customer, Alex experienced a jolt. Walking toward her was a tall striking man in his mid-thirties, with hair the color of rich brown loam.

There was something familiar about his rugged features and the set of his broad shoulders. She knew the elegant sage-green summer suit he was wearing covered a frame of hard muscle and sinew.

As he came closer to the counter, Alex gasped softly and wondered if her mind was playing tricks on her. He *had* to be the same man she'd seen at the Arabian horse show outside Reno last year. Grass Valley was only an hour and a half away, so she and her friend Sally had driven there for the weekend. While they gazed longingly at the various horses in the show ring, she had noticed a man in Western dress riding a snowy white Arabian. The horse's name, she recalled, was Domino, but she'd missed hearing the man's, since there was such a burst of applause when the horse and rider were announced. Both had stood out from the others; she'd found the man every bit as splendid as his animal.

When he'd cantered near the place where she stood with Sally, she'd caught sight of his hard-boned features and dark brown eyes beneath the brim of his Stetson hat. Then he was gone. Yet that picture of him had remained in her mind.

She knew she was staring at him now as he stood before her in the shop, but she couldn't help it. The whiteness of his shirt emphasized his tanned complexion. His eyes were as dark and striking as she remembered. His straight black hair, longer than some might find fashionable, was brushed back from his forehead. Its uncontrived simplicity suited him. Though he looked like a man who could be the CEO of some high-powered corporation, she knew he had to live the greater portion of his life outdoors; she sensed somehow that he'd never tolerate being confined by four walls.

She noticed he didn't wear a wedding ring, but that wasn't really any indication of his marital status. A man as attractive as he was had to be married, but that wouldn't prevent women from being drawn to him. It would take someone exceptional, however, to capture his attention, let alone his heart. Alex envied that woman—which was an odd reaction, considering she really knew nothing about him apart from his sensual appeal.

Oddly enough he, too, was staring at her with total absorption. She felt his gaze like a warm summer breeze, teasing the down of her fair skin and wandering to her hair, which she'd tied back with a green velvet ribbon.

"Good morning," she said at last. "May I help you?"

"I hope so," he murmured in a resonant tone she could feel to her toes. Taken at face value, his words certainly weren't threatening, yet her senses picked up something that told her to tread carefully, though she couldn't have explained why. A film of perspiration broke out on her body.

CHAPTER TWO

"WHAT EXACTLY do you have in mind?" she asked in a quiet voice.

His mouth twitched in amusement, which only added to his very male charm, and to her chagrin, Alex felt herself respond. "From time to time I run ads in various trade magazines, but I haven't been that happy with the work. Someone told me about the Write Set-Up, so I thought I'd stop by and look at some of the ads you've done for other clients."

Though he spoke in a straightforward, businesslike manner, she had the strangest impression that his mind was on something else. His eyes made a sweeping assessment of her body, lingering on the curving line of her hip covered by her wraparound skirt. Men never bothered to hide the fact that they found her attractive. In her teens she'd hated it, but with maturity she'd come to accept that her face and figure, not to mention her hair, would always attract attention.

While she worked around the house, Troy continually pestered her for photographs to "stay in practice," as he put it, while his leg healed. He said she had such good bones and coloring, she ought to make her fortune modeling. But Alex laughed at such a ridiculous notion, unable to imagine anything worse than purposely drawing attention to herself. Even now she fidgeted uncomfortably because this man's interest seemed too intimate and personal. What made it worse was her own intense attraction to him, which made *his* interest more difficult to dismiss. Already he'd thrown her off balance, and she felt as if she'd suddenly lost her bearings.

"Here are some samples." She reached under the counter for a binder containing her best typesetting work and handed it to him, trying not to be overwhelmed by her involuntary reaction to him.

He spent longer than most clients surveying the contents, then lifted his head and flicked her a searching glance. "Is this all you have to show me?"

The question meant he found her work less than satisfactory and her spirits fell. "Didn't you see anything you liked?"

One corner of his mouth lifted, softening the blow. "What I had in mind was using a photograph as the focal point of a full-page ad, and I don't see that kind of work among these samples, excellent as they are."

"Oh," she exclaimed, trying to keep the excitement out of her voice. "I keep those ads separate from the others. Just a minute." She reached underneath the counter once more and produced another binder. This one contained the full-sized ads with photos she and Troy had worked on together. Clients paid a great deal more for ads requiring color transparencies, but she had the impression this man didn't count the cost if he found what he wanted.

"Is this what you're looking for?" She opened it to the first page, which showed an attractive, long-haired man on a motorcycle. He wore a pair of leather boots manufactured in Reno. Troy had spent a long time capturing just the right angle and mood. The ad now had nationwide distribution in several Western-apparel catalogs.

The man looked at the picture, then raised his dark head and studied her features with disarming intensity. "I've seen this ad before. It's good."

The compliment, however well-intentioned, left her feeling uneasy. It was as if he'd been forced to admit something against his will.

Another client entered the shop to pick up some work, and she dealt with him while the enigmatic man at the counter slowly thumbed through the rest of the ads.

When they were alone once more, her gaze went to the book, which lay open at the last ad. The photo was of a very masculine specimen running a jackhammer. He was shirtless, and displayed a well-defined chest and biceps. A romance writer from Sparks had wanted the ad for some bookmarks to help sell her novel, *Black Jack and the Debutante.*

The photo would definitely grab a woman's attention. Alex had to admit her brother did great work and had caught the essence of the man's appeal on camera. Personally, though, she didn't care for that kind of advertising.

Although, she mused, unable to suppress a small smile, if the model had been the man standing in front of her, she'd probably have to reassess her thinking and keep several bookmarks for herself—one for her purse, another for the refrigerator door, possibly one for her bathroom mirror and definitely one for her bedside table.

After a few minutes, the stranger closed the book and eyed her steadily. "You've done a wide variety of publicity shots. I can understand why my friend recommended you. Let's see what you can do with this."

He pulled a two-by-three-inch glossy from the inside pocket of his suit jacket and handed it to her. Before she could catch herself she cried out, "That's Domino! I saw you riding him at the show near Reno last Fourth of July! He had the most beautiful silver mane and tail I've ever seen."

Something flared briefly in the man's eyes. "You were there?"

"I love horses, Arabians especially, and I try to attend any shows in the area." An unguarded smile illuminated her face. "Yours was absolutely magnificent! He's of Polish stock, isn't he?"

He gave an almost imperceptible nod. "I see you know your horseflesh. Ms...."

"Duncan," Alex offered nervously, wondering what she'd said that made him sound so remote. "Domino's the reason I remembered you," she lied.

"So that's why you were staring at me when I walked in here. Domino'll be flattered when I tell him."

Redheads blush easily, and Alex was no exception, eliciting a dazzling smile from the stranger. He obviously hadn't been deceived by her lie.

In an attempt to pull herself together she said, "You looked born to the saddle, Mr...."

"Quinn. Zackery Quinn." His mouth still curved, but his eyes held an expression she couldn't decipher.

"Of course! The Circle Q Ranch in Mason Valley!" He was *that* Quinn? Probably the state's most eligible bachelor? Even people in California knew of the first Zackery Quinn, a legendary figure who'd had the foresight to buy up a good deal of the land Reno now stood on.

It was one of the largest working cattle ranches in Nevada, covering close to 100,000 acres of prime grazing land. Besides employing a small army of people, it boasted Arabian-horse stables people from all over the world came to visit.

And the man who held such a veritable empire together, the man who had expanded its holdings, the man who could afford to fly in the best ad experts from Hollywood or New York in his own company plane, had sought *her* out to do business? She didn't think so.

So why had Zackery Quinn the third—or was it the fourth—come to the Write Set-Up?

The question loomed large in her mind. Despite his charm, she had an uneasy feeling about him. Now more than ever, she suspected his motives and wondered at his presence in her small shop.

Meeting his gaze head-on, she said, "What exactly is the purpose of your ad, Mr. Quinn?"

He took the photograph from her nerveless fingers and put it back into his pocket. "I don't have time to go into it now. How late do you stay open?"

"Six o'clock."

"I have some other business affairs to take care of, but I should be back before closing to discuss the details."

Alex couldn't begin to figure him out. "Fine. I'll see you later, then."

After a brief pause he nodded and left the office. Alex immediately turned to her worktable with every intention of finishing several projects she'd promised to do by this afternoon. She should take advantage of the quiet and get busy. But the enigmatic Mr. Quinn had disrupted her peace of mind, and she had trouble settling down to work.

Around eleven, people started dropping in to order business cards and invitations. She stayed so busy that Troy fixed lunch and brought it to her. But she couldn't forget that Zackery Quinn would be coming back at the end of the day. By five-thirty her nerves made it impossible to concentrate. She gave up trying and went into the bathroom to put on a light coral lipstick and brush her hair.

Another customer came in at a quarter to six. Alex felt a curious mixture of relief and disappointment when she discovered a woman at the counter needing a passport picture. By the time her client left, it was five after six.

Without hesitation Alex locked the front door and closed the shutters, thinking tonight was definitely a night she didn't want to stay home. Maybe she'd take Troy for pizza and a movie. Anything to get her mind off the man who'd managed to infiltrate her thoughts far too easily.

As she turned off the light, she heard a rap on the door. Her pulse raced, but willing herself to stay calm, she walked to the entry and unlocked the door. When she pulled it open, he was waiting there. "I'm too late, aren't I?" he murmured.

"That's all right," she said, lying for the second time that day. But, despite her misgivings, curiosity had been consuming her; she wouldn't be able to rest until she knew the real reason for his visit. "It's only ten after six. I often stay open late for clients who can't see me any other time. It's one of the advantages—and one of the curses—of having a business in your own home," she said. "Come in."

He stepped inside, his lips curved in a slight smile. "And which heading do I fall under?"

"If I can help prepare an ad that'll make you happy, then definitely the former." She moved behind the counter, acutely aware of the tension between them, a tension that made her excited and wary at the same time.

"You look too young to be running your own business."

He didn't sound condescending, exactly. He certainly seemed to be paying her a compliment; nevertheless, she sensed that all was not right.

"I'm afraid the need to survive has no respect for age, Mr. Quinn. Shall we discuss your ad?"

He darted her a speculative look before saying, "One with a photograph, for starters. I used to show Domino in California and Oregon. But since he cut a tendon in the Santa Barbara Rancheros Ride, I'm going to use him for stud purposes only. I want to advertise in some trade magazines, and I think the right picture will say it all. I'd like to see what kind of photographs you can produce."

His proposition stunned Alex. If the offer was sincere, then this commission would be her most important to date. His endorsement of her work would mean thousands of dollars worth of free publicity. But even more important to Alex, she and Troy would be working with his famous stallion.

Arching one brow, she said, "I'm a qualified photographer and so is my brother. Troy has a natural ability, and he picked up a lot from my father, who started a portrait studio in our home years ago. But he'll only just turn eighteen in August. He's still learning. Are you sure you wouldn't prefer to go with a more experienced free-lance photographer? Someone who can do real justice to a champion like Domino?"

A brooding look darkened his features. "Are you telling me you and your brother aren't equal to the task?"

"No," she declared. "Of course not. I simply wanted you to know the facts."

"Good. I admire honesty." His voice matched the dangerous flicker of his smile, or maybe it was merely a trick of light that had made her imagine such a look. "Frankly, I want something different, and after seeing your portfolio, I think I may have found the people to do it."

Still incredulous, she asked, "Is Domino in California?"

"No. He came home from Santa Barbara last weekend. My plan is to invite you to my ranch and let you get a feel for the place. It'll give you a chance to pick a setting you think will show him to the best advantage. I know it's asking a lot when you have a busy work schedule, but in order to see some areas of the property I have in mind, we'll need the better part of a day. Naturally I'll pay you for your time."

What does he really want?

She'd wager a month's earnings that his proposition had little to do with a photograph. Intrigued in spite of herself, she said, "We'll be free Sunday, if that's convenient for you."

"Sunday it is," he said with a satisfied drawl. "Morning is a beautiful time at the ranch. Do you mind if we get an early start?"

"No, of course not."

"Would it be ruining your beauty sleep if I came by for you at five-thirty?"

"I've always been a morning person," she replied, ignoring the flattery, which she didn't trust. "Of course, Troy's a different story, but five-thirty will be fine."

"How do you handle that and late nights, too?"

She blinked. "Late nights?"

"I imagine you have a . . . social life."

Alex chose her words carefully, not sure what he meant to imply. "I don't let anything interfere with my work, Mr. Quinn."

"I'm glad to hear it." There was a suggestion of mockery in his tone. "We'll be putting in a long day."

"Troy and I will be ready."

"Do you ride?"

"Yes," she answered without hesitation, and for an instant she thought she detected surprise in his expression. "But Troy couldn't manage it right now. He has a broken leg and won't be out of his cast for a couple of months."

After a prolonged silence he said, "Horseback is the only way to really see the property, and I don't want to wait two months to get started on this project."

Now that she'd committed herself this far, she planned to go all the way, if for no other reason than to find out what Zackery Quinn really wanted.

"I'll come without him and get some location shots as we ride. Then you can look over the proofs and if there's one you particularly like, we can plan to get pictures of Domino in that spot. If the area is inaccessible by four-wheel-drive, I presume you could transport Troy by helicopter?"

He nodded. "It's obvious you know what you're talking about."

Again she had the impression that he was saying one thing and meaning another. "Photographers do whatever it takes to get the job done. Right now Troy is hampered by his leg, but he's really talented. Last year during the Christmas break, he was flown by helicopter to Donner Pass to photograph some winter scenes for a calendar put out by a California mountaineering club. You saw the photos in the binder."

"I did, and now I'm even more impressed knowing the story behind them."

For once he sounded sincere, but Alex had grown tired of trying to second-guess him. "I'll have to be home by six in the evening," she told him, worried, suddenly, that she was getting in over her head.

"Since I plan to fly you to the ranch and back," he said, "I think we can have you safely returned before whoever it is starts beating down your door."

Alex was positive Zackery Quinn never said or did anything without a purpose behind it. If, this time, he was asking about men in her life, she had no intention of satisfying his curiosity.

"I'd appreciate that," she said in a steady voice. His shrewd regard sent a little thrill of alarm through her body.

"Five-thirty it is, Ms. Duncan. Wear something comfortable and bring along a jacket. It's cool in the mornings."

Deciding to take the offensive, she smiled broadly and said, "Both Troy and I look forward to working with you and your stallion, Mr. Quinn. Thank you for giving the Write Set-Up the opportunity."

The moment he grasped her extended hand, a sensation like liquid fire raced up her arm, quickening her body. He must have felt the reaction, because one corner of his mouth curved with a sensuality that made her breath catch in her throat.

Somehow his thumb had found the pulse throbbing at her wrist and he caressed it with gentle insistence, evoking feelings deep inside that twenty-four years of living had never revealed to her. Her shocked gaze flew to his. A deep blush washed over her face and neck, and she abruptly pulled her hand free.

"Until Sunday," he said softly, his narrowed gaze dwelling on her lips for an overlong moment before he strode from the office.

Alex stood motionless behind the counter, stunned by her physical response to a man who'd been playing some kind of obscure game with her from the second he'd entered her shop. The only thing she could be absolutely certain of was the momentary flash of desire in his eyes before he turned away—and her own strange feeling of regret.

Regret that he hadn't lowered his hard beautiful mouth to hers.

IT WAS CLOSE TO TEN by the time Zack got home. After visiting his father's bedroom to check on his condition and kiss him good-night, he chatted briefly with the nurse, then took the stairs two at a time to the second floor. He walked past Randy's room, noting that the boy was still awake; he could hear the TV through the closed door.

At last he headed for his bedroom on the third floor. Jerking off his suit jacket and tie, he unfastened the top buttons of his shirt, then poured himself a scotch from the cabinet in the adjoining sitting room. While he drained the glass, he pulled some of the posters from the box he'd shoved into one corner and laid them out on the coffee table.

His preoccupation with his father's first stroke which had come shortly after Wendie's death must have been the reason he hadn't noticed Alexandria Duncan at the Reno horse show. With that flaming red hair, she was a hell of a lot more beautiful than any woman had a right to be. And Alexandria Duncan was nobody's fool. The second he'd introduced himself as Zackery Quinn, she'd connected him with the Circle Q. Did she also know that he and Andrew Cordell were related, that the governor's wife had been Zack's sister, Wendie? *That Randy was their son?*

The Quinn name had always been prominent in the state, and most people knew of his relationship to the governor. The more Zack thought about it, the more he wondered if there could be an elaborate scheme in play here, possibly with the aim of embarrassing Andrew and preventing his reelection.

Maybe Ms. Duncan had been given inside information from someone at the mansion—someone who had it in for Andrew and knew of Randy's propensity for getting into trouble. Someone who knew of his passion for ham radio.

Zack couldn't think of anything more damaging to Andrew's reputation than the revelation that his teenaged son was involved in an illegal operation—one that might even have its roots in pornography.

Or maybe the plan was to get Randy well and truly involved, then try to blackmail Andrew by threatening exposure. Randy's problems were well-known at the mansion, particularly his bout with drugs that had landed him in a Texas hospital for three months.

If that was the case, then someone had done his or her research extremely well. On the other hand, Zack wondered if he was jumping to conclusions, trying to prove a tie-in to Andrew that didn't exist. Maybe it was pure coincidence that Randy, of all people, just happened to get on the same air wave with Troy and become embroiled in this latest mess.

Which brought Zack's thoughts full circle. *Alexandria Duncan.* What part did she play? Was she another pawn, or did she orchestrate the—

"Uncle Zack? I heard you come up here."

His nephew's voice jolted him back to his surroundings. Zack turned his head to see a nervous looking Randy standing in the doorway. The expression "as easy as taking candy from a baby" came to Zack's mind every time he thought about the boy's naïveté.

What man, young or old, could be blamed for fantasizing about a woman like Alexandria Duncan? He had no trouble understanding why a bunch of hormone-driven seventeen-year-olds were salivating over her pictures. Zack had seen her in the flesh and felt the pull of her attraction, and it disturbed him a great deal more than he cared to admit.

"Did you find out anything?"

"I met the lady," he muttered, "but I've got to know more before I can make a final judgment. That's where you come in. I'm going to need your cooperation."

"Sure." Randy was quick to respond and more penitent than Zack had ever seen him.

"Ms. Duncan is coming out to the ranch on Sunday to spend the day with me riding around the property." Randy's eyes grew huge.

"It's part of my plan to get a confession from her. Since I don't want her to see you, you'll have to stay indoors while she's with me. Will that be a problem?''

"Heck, no. I love spending time with Grandpa. Sometimes I think he's the only person who understands me."

Zack eyed his nephew soberly. After Wendie's death, when both Zack and Andrew had been so torn by their own grief, Randy had turned to his grandfather for comfort. They'd become inseparable. "Now you know why I hang around Dad so much, Randy. I guess he's about the best listener in the entire world."

Randy nodded. "You're pretty good at it yourself, Uncle Zack. When you're not busy trying to keep me out of trouble," he added sheepishly.

Some of the tension eased out of Zack. "Coming from you, that's a real compliment. So, are you up to flying to Carson City in the morning?" Randy nodded. "Good. As soon as we get you home, you'll contact Troy over the radio and tell him the whole operation has to be put on hold because you have to join your parents on vacation.

"If he tries to get more details, you tell him that you're leaving for the airport and won't be available to discuss anything until you get back in July. It'll be a lie, but he'll never know the difference."

A puzzled frown creased Randy's forehead. "Why don't I just phone him from here?"

"Because he knows you have to leave from Carson City, and it'll be more believable if you contact him over the radio, since that's what you've always done in the past. I want to hear his reaction when he finds out you're going on a trip and won't be available.

Maybe he'll give something away that'll help me figure out what's really going on. You'll have to make contact with Steve, as well, and tell him the same story."

Randy's bleak expression aroused Zack's compassion and he tousled his nephew's hair. "Hey, it's going to be all right. We're on to Troy and his sister, and this thing is going to backfire in their faces."

"I really don't think his sister's involved . . ."

"Well, we'll find out for sure."

"I hope so."

"Don't you trust your uncle Zack?"

"Yeah, actually I do." Then his face fell. "Are you going to tell Dad? The thing is, I never meant to hurt him," he murmured, looking close to tears.

Zack studied his nephew. "I believe you, Randy. That's why I'm handling this on my own."

"Thanks. I owe you—for a lot of things."

"No, you don't. We're family and we stick together. If I was in trouble, I bet you'd be the first one to help me."

A hint of a smile appeared. "You know I would. The only problem is, you never do anything stupid. Mom used to say you could sense trouble a mile off."

Amused and saddened, Zack explained, "I think she was being a bit ironic—talking about my bachelor status. In her zeal to see me married, she chose to overlook my imperfections and ignore certain events in my past I'm not particularly proud of."

"Really?" Randy stared at Zack in amazement.

Zack nodded. "Another time when it's not so late, I'll tell you about them. You're old enough to hear the truth. Maybe then you'll understand why I don't want history repeating itself." He paused. "I love you, Randy."

"You really mean that?" the boy asked. His voice had a betraying tremor.

"How can you doubt it? You're as close to a son as I'm ever going to have."

Randy looked incredulous. "That's crazy! You could marry any one of a dozen women tomorrow and have all the children you want. Man, I'd kill to have them swarm around me the way they do around you."

His nephew's lack of confidence was even greater than Zack had realized. No wonder he consistently sought attention, negative or otherwise. Zack put a gentle hand on the boy's shoulder. "There's something you need to know, Randy. Marriage isn't for me." His voice hardened as he spoke. "That's why I'm pinning all my hopes on you."

A solemn look passed between them. "You're serious, aren't you?" said Randy.

Zack nodded. "Completely. So I guess there's nothing I wouldn't do for you if I could. One day when I'm gone, the Circle Q will be yours—to keep or to sell."

"*To sell?* When it means everything to you? And to Grandpa?" Randy raised startled eyes to his uncle. "No way!"

Zack felt an overwhelming relief at Randy's reaction. "Well, that's why I want to teach you about ranching this summer." *And hope you learn to love it with the same passion I do,* Zack mused. Nothing put life into perspective better than gazing up at the end-

less sky, running your hand along a fence your ancestors had built, breathing the pine-scented mountain
breeze of the Sierras. "What do you say we call it a
night so we can get an early start in the morning?"

In an unexpected gesture, Randy gave him a hug,
then ran lightly from the bedroom. After closing the
door, Zack wandered over to the coffee table and put
the pictures back in the box. But not until he'd studied the woman's face one more time. Long before
Andrew returned from Asia, Zack determined, the
truth about her would be revealed and she'd be out of
the mail-order business for good. And any other
"business" she happened to be involved in. There
might even be criminal charges filed.

Yes, he had plans for Ms. Duncan, plans he'd talked
over with Miguel at lunch earlier in the day. A cruel
smile broke out on Zack's face. Alone, on an inaccessible area of the ranch, he'd wring any guilty secrets
from those provocative lips and make damn sure she
never flaunted her considerable assets before a camera or an audience again.

If she *had* been hired by someone else, then she'd
probably been working in one of the hotel floor shows,
probably under an assumed name. But could he track
down that kind of information?

A woman who performed half-naked would probably agree to do almost anything if there was enough
money in it. Even work at a typesetting business during the day to establish a legitimate front, he thought
wryly.

Miguel agreed she could have quite the operation
going. Pin-up calendars for men and milder forms of

the same pictures for teens. Something innocent enough not to raise eyebrows, yet enticing enough to bring in $20,000 in less than three months.

According to what Troy had told Randy, his sister had great business savvy. She had brains, plus beauty, and that innocent act was pure Oscar material. Miguel, too, believed she was behind the scheme, deliberately using her younger brother not only to do much of the work but to provide a smokescreen for her own, more lucrative plans.

She'd played her part carefully, not showing too much eagerness to spend a day on the ranch, yet in the end she'd agreed to come. Miguel had warned Zack that she'd probably try to exploit him in some way now that he'd entered the picture. Quinn money was no doubt an added incentive.

But on that score Zack was way ahead of his friend. He looked forward to foiling her efforts with a vehemence that surprised even him. He'd make her sorry she ever got entangled with him or the Cordell family....

CHAPTER THREE

"N6AFW. N6AFW. THIS IS N6HUT calling."

"This is N6AFW. Hey, Jerry? How're you doing? I thought you were at your relatives' place. I've been expecting a phone call. Did you get the stuff?"

"Yeah. It came yesterday."

"Were you able to keep it a secret from them?"

Randy's unsmiling gaze darted to Zack, who stood by the table where Randy kept his equipment. "No sweat. No one was around when the delivery van arrived."

"That's great, because Tuesday you're going to get a triple load of posters. They'll be coming in a couple of big boxes, so be extra careful."

"Did you say triple?" Randy swallowed hard.

"Yeah. Sunday, Alex is going out on a photo session and she'll be gone all day, which means I'll have the place to myself and I can get three times the work done. You're going to love the latest poster. She's got a new bathing suit on. It's *great!*" Randy eyed his uncle guiltily.

First the innocent poses, now they were down to the bathing suit. What next?

Zack's features hardened in distaste. It didn't take a brilliant mind to deduce that before very long the tempting Ms. Duncan would allow herself to be photographed without the benefit of clothes. He fought to erase certain mental images from his mind and nodded to his nephew to carry on.

"Th-that's great about the posters, Troy, but you'd better hold on to them for a while because my...my parents decided I have to join them on their trip. I'm going to the airport in a few minutes. I won't be back for three weeks, so this'll be my last chance to contact you before I leave."

"*Three weeks?*" The disappointment in Troy's voice made Randy shift his weight uneasily. "I thought you didn't want to be with your family."

Zack had it in his heart to feel sorry for Randy, who was struggling to make appropriate responses without letting on that anything was wrong.

"I don't, but Dad is insisting, and there isn't anything I can do about it."

"That's tough. But don't worry. Steve and I will look after things while you're gone. There's this guy who's got the hots for Alex, and he's going to get me a Japanese ham magazine from some other guy who travels a lot between here and Tokyo and buys auto parts from him.

"He thinks it'll get him in good with Alex, but between you and me, he doesn't stand a chance. She's a horse lover and has this dream of marrying a big rancher so she can ride to her heart's content. The auto-parts dude doesn't quite fit the bill, if you know what I mean," he finished with a chuckle.

At that revelation Zack's eyes narrowed to slits. Randy saw the look and swallowed hard. "Yeah, I read you."

"Actually, I feel sorry for the dude. But I'm not telling him he was never in the running until after he gets me that magazine. I'm expecting it any day, and I'll be able to get a lot of addresses out of it. By the time you get back, we might even have some orders."

"Look, Troy, maybe you ought to wait on that until I'm home."

"Hey, don't worry about not helping out. What are friends for? You'd do the same for me if I couldn't carry on my part for a while. We're in this business together, right?"

"Right," Randy muttered into the mike.

"I'll call Steve and tell him what you told me. We'll manage things fine until you're home again. By the way, where are you going?"

Zack shook his head so Randy wouldn't give Troy any useful information. "C-Canada."

"You're lucky! While you're there, why not pick up some local call signs and we can start sending catalogs to the Canadians?"

Randy hesitated before saying, "I don't know that I'll have that kind of time, Troy. Dad and...Mom have plans." He saw Zack's nod of approval at the blatant lie.

"Well, try, anyway. Have a good trip. I've never been farther away than Disneyland. Your dad must make a good living to be able to afford to take your whole family up there. That's what I want to do some day. Make a lot of money so I can go wherever I want."

Randy's guilty glance swerved to Zack. "Yeah. I know what you mean."

"Call me when you get back. Steve and I ought to have good news for you. This is N6HUT signing off."

"This is N6AFW. Over and out." After turning off the unit, Randy said, "I tried to put him off, Uncle Zack."

"I know you did. Don't worry, I'll take care of everything from here on out," Zack vowed with a dangerous glint in his eye. "Let's head back to the ranch."

"TROY?" ALEX POKED her head inside the door of his room. Her brother lay there dead to the world. "Troy?" she repeated.

Finally he stirred. "Yeah?"

"I'm going to be picked up any minute. Don't forget that the Olsons are driving you to church at nine-thirty, and afterward they're taking you back to their house for lunch. I've ironed your dress shirt. It's hanging on the back of the bathroom door."

He shot up in bed and brushed the hair out of his eyes. "I thought you weren't going to treat me like a baby anymore. It's my business if I go to church or not. I noticed you didn't ask my permission if *you* could skip church today."

Alex fought to control her temper. "Okay. So what do you plan to do all day?"

"I'll think of something. I always do." The front buzzer sounded, leaving her no time to discuss the issue further.

"I've got to go, but I'll be back by dinner. Please call the Olsons later, then, and tell them not to come. Be sure to thank them for the invitation."

"You know something, Alex? You're worse than a mom."

His comment shouldn't have hurt, but it did. She knew what he meant. She also knew he was depressed, or he wouldn't want to stay home all day by himself. If something didn't change soon, she'd have to seek professional help for Troy.

By the time she slipped on her leather jacket and collected her camera case, another minute had passed. She dashed to the front door and unlocked it, hoping all traces of her tears were gone. "Good morning, Mr. Quinn. I'm sorry you had to wait. I had some last-minute instructions to give my brother." She shut and locked the door behind her.

In the shadowy morning light, his chiseled features were less distinct, yet once again she felt drawn to him. His tall powerful physique was defined by snug-fitting denim jeans and a dark shirt. Well-worn cowboy boots added another inch to his already commanding height. Even though she, too, was in boots, he dwarfed her five-foot-seven frame.

"Take more time if you need it." His voice sounded lower than she remembered. She liked its husky tone, which seemed to resonate in the early-morning air and wrap itself intimately around her.

"No. I'm all set."

He relieved her of her camera case and, without a word, closed his hand over her elbow and ushered her to the station wagon parked in front of the house.

They accidentally brushed against each other as they walked, and each brief contact sent that same hot trickle of fire through her body.

Her gaze darted to the Circle Q insignia painted on the door he held open for her. She climbed in, conscious of his gaze, then watched in fascination as he put the case in the back and slid behind the wheel.

She leaned back against the seat, refraining from comment. Something about his presence and the peaceful calm of the early morning made her want to savor the moment. For whatever reason he, too, seemed disinclined to say anything. Right now she chose to forget that he was hiding something from her and concentrated, instead, on the beauty of the day as they drove through her neighborhood toward the highway. It wasn't until they approached the small airport that he spoke.

"You're so quiet I have to wonder if you're not feeling well. Or are you afraid of flying?"

Her lips curved upward in a genuine smile. "Neither one. To be honest, this is my favorite time of day. The air's still fresh and everything's just starting to come alive." She paused. "I'm so excited to be visiting your ranch I feel like a schoolgirl on her first day of summer vacation."

She had no idea what he might have said in response because they'd reached the Circle Q hangar. He alighted from the car to come around and assist her.

She reached for her camera case, slinging the strap over her shoulder as he escorted her to the gleaming yellow twin-engine plane with the brown Circle Q insignia on the tail.

Feeling a sense of unreality, Alex climbed in after him. He relieved her of her case while she sat in the copilot's seat and strapped herself in.

He raised an eyebrow. "Something tells me you've done this before."

"Several times." She nodded. "My best friend's father is a crop duster from Marysville. Sally and I went along for the ride whenever he allowed it." But his plane hadn't looked anything like this, Alex mused. She could scarcely comprehend such luxury.

Though her family had been a happy one, her hardworking mother and father barely made enough money to pay the bills. Alex had been forced to dream about the things she secretly wanted but could never have. Like a horse of her own.... She sighed, shaking off the thought. Deep down, she understood Troy's need to earn more than minimum wage. It came from a lifetime of watching every penny.

He'd done gardening and cut lawns as soon as he could handle a mower. And Alex had been the neighborhood baby-sitter. If she or her brother wanted a bike or a new dress or a football, they had to earn the money to buy it themselves.

"Since you don't seem nervous," her companion said after putting on his headphones, "I'll give you a tour of the ranch before we land. Perhaps you'll see a spot that captures your artistic eye."

With his dark winged brows drawn together in concentration, he spoke to the tower, then turned the plane toward the east. Before long they were airborne in a pale blue sky, no sign of a cloud on the horizon.

It seemed as if they hadn't been up ten minutes before he informed her they were flying southeast over the ranch and she saw the incredible lush green of Mason Valley unfold below. He pointed out fields of alfalfa, wheat and soybeans, dotted by sheds and barns and farm equipment.

He flew low over pastureland where thousands of Herefords, tended by border collies and stockmen on horseback, grazed contentedly. And what had been a silvery ribbon at a higher elevation turned out to be Walker River, which flowed through his property. In places it appeared a hundred feet across.

At one point her stomach seemed to turn over as he performed an expert maneuver, dipping the wing of the plane to make it possible for her to pick out details along the bank. Dozens of picturesque spots that would make perfect backdrops for a photograph of Domino flashed before her.

"It's so beautiful," she said breathlessly as she lifted wondering eyes to discover his intent gaze fastened on her. Was that a look of enmity she saw? It was only there for a moment, but she was sure she hadn't imagined it.

Bewildered and hurt because she'd thought they were sharing a special moment, she turned her head and focused on the view ahead. But the joy had gone out of her day. All her earlier suspicions that he had a hidden motive in inviting her to his ranch had just been confirmed.

The plane droned on toward the eastern escarpment of the Sierra Nevada's dotted with sagebrush, clumps of cottonwood and pine growing from the rich, dark brown soil, the color of which reminded her of his hair. The sheer size and natural beauty of everything she saw brought him forcefully to mind—a man of inherent authority and intelligence, at one with this Western kingdom he'd been destined to rule.

She smoothed a wisp of hair from her forehead. More than ever, she wanted to know what had driven him to seek her out. She was determined to have some answers before the day's end.

"Have you seen enough to decide where you'd like to ride this morning?"

Jerked from her troubled thoughts, she replied, "The river has intriguing possibilities, but so do some of the meadows climbing the escarpment. What about you?" She gave him a direct gaze. "I assume you have a few favorite spots of your own. Maybe some secret place you loved as a boy?"

"I had dozens of them, because everything about the ranch delighted me," Zack murmured, and then realized what he'd said.

"Let's start with the first dozen," she suggested. "Maybe there's a still pool in the river where the heavy blossoms of a flowering fruit tree are mirrored," she said dreamily. Averting her eyes, she continued, "I can picture Domino in such a setting. On a ranch of this magnitude and splendor, there must be many beautiful hidden spots only the owner would know about."

In the distance she could see the landing strip, and she marveled at the ease with which he maneuvered the aircraft for the descent. "It sounds as if there's a budding poet inside the businesswoman."

His tone held an edge of sarcasm, and Alex was unaccountably stung. "Only when the surroundings inspire it," she retorted.

He turned in her direction, his lips quirked in irony. "I'm looking forward to discovering what other hidden facets surface before our day comes to an end."

He set down the plane as gently as a dandelion seed drifting with the breeze. "Welcome to the Circle Q, Ms. Duncan. We aim to please." He removed his headgear, giving her another glimpse of his heart-stopping smile. When he did that, she could forget he had any other face—or any other motive than the one he had stated.

In a matter of seconds, he'd helped her from the plane and they were walking the short distance to a pickup truck parked alongside the strip. "It's a shame your brother couldn't ride with us this morning," he said once they were seated inside. "It's going to be a beautiful day for taking pictures. Considering his photographic skills, why haven't I heard about your business before?"

"Because we only moved here from Grass Valley three months ago," she murmured, noting the cleanliness of his nails against the dark tan of his hands. It disturbed her that she was so aware of everything about him when they were scarcely more than strangers.

"What made you move to Nevada?" He inserted the key in the ignition but didn't turn it on, apparently waiting for her reply.

"Troy and I both love the Tahoe area and there are more business opportunities in Reno than Grass Valley. We can always go home for visits—it's only an hour and a half away."

"I'll bet your brother misses his friends."

His comment hurt because lately Alex had been thinking the same thing and wondering if the move was, in part, responsible for Troy's depression. "I'm sure he does, but I had hoped new surroundings would ease the pain of losing our parents. They were killed in a train crash three years ago, and Troy was particularly close to Dad. They shared an interest in photography."

He turned toward her. "I'm sorry about your loss."

Though his tone was appropriately compassionate, his bold eyes sent another message. They wandered over her luxuriant hair, tied back at the nape with a ribbon, then fell on the flushed curve of her cheek and slightly upturned nose.

The fullness of her lips held his gaze for a moment, then his eyes traveled lower to the creamy skin of her throat and the curves beneath her jacket. His almost insolent appraisal created a heat in her body that had nothing to do with the warmth of the cab.

"I have no doubt that with all your qualifications, you'll do well here in Nevada." He turned away and started the engine.

She frowned. "I'm not sure I understand what you mean."

"I was referring to your photographic and typesetting expertise. What did you think I meant?"

Alex didn't have an answer, but again she wondered about his reasons for bringing her to his ranch. Forcing a smile, she said, "Well, if the head of the

Circle Q is pleased with the shoot, then Troy and I will certainly be grateful for any publicity it generates."

"I imagine you've attracted more than your fair share already."

Her head whipped around. "More?"

"A beautiful business woman must perform quite a balancing act between her clients and suitors."

"I'd say a handsome rancher has much the same problem," she returned, not wanting him to know how little she'd dated since dropping out of university. Raising a brother, plus handling their finances, hadn't left a lot of time for a social life.

"If you knew anything about ranching, you'd realize the two situations aren't synonymous at all," he said smoothly as he revved the engine. "Since I'm paying for your photographic expertise, I suggest we get on with it." He put the truck into gear and floored the accelerator. Alex had to swallow the angry retort that sprang to her lips.

With little apparent concern for her comfort, he drove along the dirt track at breakneck speed. She couldn't imagine their achieving any sort of harmony after this.

Based on various disparaging remarks he'd made about women, she was convinced that Zack Quinn— a man who seemed to have everything most of the world coveted—had been hurt by a woman years before. Hurt so badly, he'd never gotten over it.

From now on, she'd behave like a consummate professional and not let his hostility affect her. One thing she did know about him—he loved his land and his horses. She'd concentrate on that and create a series of photographs that would immortalize Domino.

Oddly enough, this was one project she wanted to do without Troy's help. For the first time, she wished she could claim that little spark of genius for herself.

"In case you hadn't noticed, we've arrived. The horses are eager for a workout. Yours is ready and waiting."

She'd been too deep in thought to realize they'd pulled up to the stable, where a bay mare stood saddled in the paddock. A couple of stablehands waved and shouted greetings to their boss.

Alex grabbed her camera case and jumped down from the truck. She could hardly wait to mount the mare he'd chosen for her and headed in its direction. Nearby stood a magnificent chestnut. The animal snorted at her approach and lunged farther away, every bit as proud and arrogant as its master.

The bay, however, responded to her crooning and stepped forward to let Alex her rub her nose. Then she tried to reach Alex's pocket. "How did you know I'd brought you a present?" The bay rewarded her question with a gentle neigh.

Alex raised a smiling face to her enigmatic host, who stood staring at her as if he'd never seen her before. "She's a very intelligent animal. See?" She pulled a lump of sugar from her jacket pocket and let the horse take it off her hand. "What's her name?" Alex called over her shoulder.

"Gum Drop."

Alex chuckled. "That's a perfect name but not very dignified. I suppose your stallion has a more majestic one—El Kadid or something?"

His lips twitched. "Close. He's Ali Pasha III, but answers to Pasha."

"Will he accept sugar from me?"

He shrugged. "Not likely, but let's find out." He gave an ear-splitting whistle. The stallion tossed his head in the air, pawed the ground with a foreleg and came running. Alex gasped.

"Easy, Pasha." He gentled the horse with soothing words and then nodded to Alex, who moved closer and extended her hand beneath the stallion's flared nostrils.

Pasha reared back and galloped off, but returned several times to sniff at the sugar. But he still refused to touch it.

"Smart boy," Zack muttered in a low voice. Alex heard him and couldn't resist the challenge.

"Pasha . . . Pasha . . . come to me, Pasha. Come on, fella." She used her silkiest tone. "You'd like some sugar, wouldn't you? Come on, you beauty. I know you. You're just a marshmallow underneath."

Finally, when the bay tried to move in, the stallion snatched the sugar away and galloped off to enjoy the sweet in private. "I'll be darned," one of the stablehands muttered in disbelief. "I've never seen him do that before, boss."

"We live and learn, Pete." The caustic remark deflated her small triumph. For reasons she hadn't yet examined, she wanted to win over the big stallion. Maybe it was simply to best Zack Quinn—or maybe it was to show him she could be trusted. She didn't want to be constantly on guard against him, not when she was spending a whole day on the Circle Q riding Gum Drop. It was like a dream come true.

Ever since childhood, she'd wanted a horse. She and Sally were both horse-crazy, and when they did spend any of her hard-earned baby-sitting money, they generally went horseback riding at a local stable.

"Here, let me help you with that, ma'am." The man called Pete fastened a canteen and the strap of her camera to Gum Drop's pommel while Alex swung her leg over. Out of the corner of her eye she watched Zack saddle the stallion, then mount him in one fluid movement.

"Ready?" he asked a few seconds later as his horse sidled next to hers. "You'd better wear this or the sun will scorch that tender skin." He reached over to place a broad-brimmed hat on her head. His hands brushed her warm cheeks as he lowered the tie in place beneath her chin.

Maybe she was mistaken, but she thought his fingers lingered for a moment against her throat. She was sure he could feel the wild beating of her pulse. Alex wished she could control, or at least conceal, her reactions.

"Thank you." The words came out a mere whisper. Against her will, her eyes traveled to his sun-bronzed face, framed by dark, breeze-tossed hair. "Aren't you going to wear one?"

Their gazes fused. "I find that hats tend to be a nuisance. But on occasion—" His mouth twisted ironically "—they have their uses."

Alex refused to let him spoil an otherwise wonderful morning. Ignoring the mockery in those penetrating eyes, she opened her case and pulled out her camera. She'd put in a fresh roll of high-speed color film before leaving home. She made the necessary adjustments, then started taking pictures of everything in sight, which included her host and his stockmen. Today might be her only opportunity to preserve memories of the ranch. And of him...

"Pete," she heard him call out, "we'll ride to the eagle's nest and stop in the forest for lunch, in case you need to get hold of me."

"Right, boss."

So he did have a few favorite spots. Alex hugged the knowledge to herself.

The public knew one side of Zackery Quinn—the wealthy rancher who moved in exalted circles that included the governor of the state.

But Alex wanted to see the man beneath the veneer. That was the man who intrigued her, the man she desperately wanted to know.

Would she find any trace of vulnerability, or had something so traumatic happened in his past that he'd learned to suppress his emotions? Was Zackery Quinn a man beyond feeling?

CHAPTER FOUR

THE ALFALFA WAS IN BLOOM, filling the air with a sweet fragrance more intoxicating to Alex than French perfume. Mile after mile of tiny purple blossoms nestled against their dark green leaves, giving Mason Valley its reputation as one of the most fertile spots in the state. No backdrop could provide a better foil for Domino's snowy-white perfection.

Alex's spontaneous exclamations of delight brought the first hint of a response to Zack's lips, softening the severity of his inscrutable expression.

As they rode further, the terrain changed. With her camera, she captured the rich variety of sand, sage and wildflowers in riotous color, their miraculous pinks and yellows a brilliant contrast to the fields of garlic and onion under cultivation.

How she'd love to capture Domino and his owner in such a setting, with black thunderheads billowing behind them at the onset of a storm. She could picture the desert wind lifting the dark hair from his bronzed forehead, his stallion's silver mane and tail flying in the same disarray.

But the intense heat of the late-morning sun made nonsense of her imaginings, and it became an effort to keep pace with him as their horses took them up the slope of a mountain. They left the cool shade of the Russian olive trees bordering the river to enter the world of piñon pine. Almost to the eagle's nest, Alex couldn't resist turning in the saddle to survey the valley below.

"Now I understand Van Gogh's fascination with haystacks," she murmured as she snapped a series of pictures. The golden mounds dotting the peaceful green landscape fanned out like a range of rolling hills, layer upon layer. And beyond that, stretched the thousands of acres of cattle range she'd viewed from the plane.

The vast beauty of the terrain explained Zackery Quinn as nothing else could have. Only an extraordinary man, a man of power and vision, could achieve such success and inspire the kind of loyalty from his employees to hold all this together and keep it thriving. So far she'd only met a couple of the stablehands, but the friendliness and warmth they showed their boss was obviously unfeigned.

Suddenly he spoke. "If you'll concentrate on that speck in the sky circling above your head, you might get something on film you hadn't anticipated."

Alex looked up in time to see a lone bald eagle spiraling toward its nest in the rocks above. Automatically she adjusted the lens of her camera and snapped one picture after another, marveling at the bird's broad wingspan and the intelligence shining from those yellow eyes. Her breath caught as the great bird—at least a yard from wing tip to wing tip—came to perch and stood there, regarding them imperiously from above.

"He's magnificent," she whispered in awe.

"He's a *she,*" he replied.

"Oh," she said in surprise. "Where's her mate?"

When he turned his head, she glimpsed a look of icy disdain, which shattered any notion she might have had that he was enjoying her company. "She doesn't have one."

"Why?" Puzzlement darkened the blue of her eyes.

"She's a bird of prey who obviously enjoys the thrill of the chase too much to settle down to a monogamous life."

Alex realized he wasn't talking about the eagle anymore; she'd grown tired of his veiled remarks and innuendos.

"Surely, then, she's an aberration."

"Is she?" he asked in a heavily sarcastic voice, his eyes narrowed on her face. Alex's fingers tightened involuntarily on the reins.

"Of course she is! Otherwise how do you account for the survival of the species? From what I understand, when they do mate, it's for life."

A forbidding slash of brow gave him a menacing expression. "Haven't you heard? They're an endangered species. It may not be long before they're extinct," he said bleakly. Then, without warning, he changed his tone. "I suppose if I don't feed you soon, you might faint on me."

"I have to admit I am hungry."

"Then let's go. There's a place I'd like you to see before we return to the stable." She followed his lead to the valley below and soon they came to the beginnings of a small forest, so dense with cottonwood and white birch she couldn't see through it.

Curious to know what he wanted to show her, she stayed close behind him, letting her horse set the pace through the grasses and sagebrush covering the forest floor. As they penetrated its hidden depths, she had the feeling they'd entered a secret world.

She gasped in sheer delight when they came to the heart of the wood, where wild roses overflowed with a profusion of luminescent pink petals, as exotic as any flowers growing in a tropical rain forest. Their abundance spilled forth, illuminated by a few stray sunbeams that had managed to filter through the leafy canopy above.

As if on cue, the two of them dismounted and Alex pushed back her hat, letting it dangle at her back. She gazed spellbound at her surroundings, then stared at Zack for a long moment. "So this is your secret place. You knew all along it would be the perfect spot to photograph Domino."

He paused in the process of laying out their picnic on a blanket and flashed her an unreadable glance. "What lingers in a child's memory sometimes bears little resemblance to reality. I was curious to find out if the briars had taken over."

His mercurial moods baffled her. Part of the time his manner was cold and cryptic. Then unexpectedly, like now, he would share something intimate with her. She couldn't begin to understand the man. Yet her curiosity about him was insatiable. "So you've stayed away from here all these years. Why?"

"Because I've never wanted anything to destroy one of my happiest childhood memories—a time when my father was in his prime and my mother was still alive. When my sister was happy and healthy..."

"I can understand your feelings," she said almost in a whisper. "I have some cherished family memories, too. Did you used to come here for picnics?"

He nodded, a faraway look in his eyes. "My father hid my first pony here, and then pretended that I'd found it by accident. He said I could keep it."

In a few words, Zackery Quinn had told her how he felt about his father.

"What a wonderful gift," she said in an awed gentle tone. "Is your father still alive?"

"Yes."

Something in his voice told her she'd get nothing more of a personal nature out of him right now. He motioned for her to sit down and eat, but she needed a little time to work out why he'd brought her here and why he had shared something so private. She picked up the camera and studied the angle of light on the roses. After taking a dozen photographs, she sank to her knees and bit into a thick ham-and-cheese sandwich.

Suddenly visualizing the scene in her mind's eye, she said excitedly, "I have an idea for your picture! If you can position Domino beneath that overhang of blossoms, they'll trail over his mane and create an incredible illusion of fantasy. But it'll have to be shot right away before the roses stop blooming."

"With *you* mounted on his back, I agree the picture would be sensational," he said, finishing his sandwich.

His unexpected comment made her heart do a flip-flop. Alex stopped chewing, not certain she'd heard him correctly. "What did you say?"

His eyes narrowed on her face. "You don't have to pretend to be surprised. You're a breathtaking woman, Ms. Duncan, and I'm prepared to pay your asking price. With your long legs astride Domino and all that gorgeous red hair billowing over a naked shoulder, you'll be every man's fantasy, all right. I can guarantee I'll have more responses than I could possibly accommodate."

With those words, he destroyed the image of the man she had begun to cherish. In his place was the calculating businessman who'd walked into Alex's shop one bright summer morning and made chaos of her well-ordered life. At least she finally had an answer to the question plaguing her—and she was absolutely furious.

He wanted a model for the ad, one who would pose nude!

No wonder he'd opened up to her emotionally. No wonder he'd gone to these lengths to seduce her with the beauty of his ranch. Because he wanted her softened up and amenable when he put forth his disgusting proposition! What she couldn't understand was why he had chosen *her!*

She jumped to her feet, the rest of her lunch forgotten. Cheeks flaming, she said, "I'm not a model and I haven't the faintest idea where you got the idea that I would pose, nude *or* clothed, for a picture. Certainly not from any of *my* customers! It's too bad you weren't honest from the very beginning. As it is, I've left my brother alone on a Sunday when he needed my company, and you've wasted your time.''

Instead of disconcerting him as she'd intended, her words managed to produce another mocking smile, one that bordered on a sneer and infuriated her even more.

"You disappoint me, Mr. Quinn!" she snapped. "I thought you were a real horse-lover. Domino doesn't require a female astride him to attract attention. For the kind of photo you obviously have in mind, I suggest you call a modeling agency in Reno. There ought to be any number of women willing to pose to your specifications and eager for the fee you're prepared to pay. While you're at it, ask for a platinum blonde to complement Domino, instead of a redhead. That way the pink of the roses won't clash.''

She'd barely put her hand on the pommel to mount Gum Drop when the man behind her gripped her upper arms and turned her around. Alex had trouble breathing with his face so close to hers. She could see the creases bracketing his mouth and the way the tendons stood out in his neck.

"I meant no offense, Ms. Duncan," he murmured in a deep seductive voice, his thumbs caressing the tender flesh of her arms. "Contrary to what you believe, the idea of having you pose on Domino never even occurred to me until a moment ago. I would hardly have included your brother in the invitation to visit my ranch if that had been my objective.''

After his strange behavior and the shocking assumption that she'd model for him, the logic of his words and the proximity of his hard body confused her. Without conscious thought, she lifted her head to read his expression, but the unmistakable look of desire flaring in his eyes set her limbs trembling.

"Lord..." he said on a tormented groan, and almost as if he couldn't help himself, lifted his hand to untie the black satin ribbon. It fluttered to the ground as he released her hair to his questing fingers. The sensuous gesture broke through her defenses, and she could no longer fight the weakness invading her body.

"Please let me go," she whispered, desperate to stop him before things went any further. But even as she said the words, her hands, which had been pushing him away, suddenly seemed to have a mind of their own and started to roam over his chest. She needed to feel the pounding of his heart beneath her fingers.

With a fierce intake of breath he hauled her hard against him. "You do this better than anyone I've ever known," he ground out. The violence of his response shocked her. And then his mouth trapped hers, sweeping her far beyond the normal stages of tentative kissing, demanding everything she had to give.

Crushed against his chest, she found the fresh clean scent of his masculine warmth too compelling to resist. She yielded to his demands, responding with breathtaking urgency, holding nothing back. Unable to hold anything back.

They were a man and a woman who'd come together in the most elemental of ways, bestowing the beauty of their bodies on each other and finding pleasure. For the first time, Alex exulted in being a woman, because she seemed to be everything this man desired.

He *couldn't* be the same man who'd made such a hurtful and outrageous proposition, whose bitterness over what she assumed was a troubled relationship with a woman had left him distrustful and cynical.

But he was. And she was letting him do whatever he wanted, even encouraging him. At last she called on the small portion of self-control she had left and wrenched her lips from his, drawing a muffled groan from him.

Terrified of the rising tide of desire, which threatened to sweep away all common sense, Alex summoned her strength and pushed hard against his broad shoulders. Finally he let her go without a struggle. She staggered backward, not ready for this new reality, one that left her aching for fulfillment.

With shaking fingers she smoothed back the hair he'd disheveled with his hands during their heated embrace. Avoiding his gaze, she said, "I-I've taken enough pictures of the ranch to give Troy a base from which to work and...and I need to get back to town." The words escaped in a jerky, almost incoherent stream.

"You're sure?" came the challenge, one she chose to ignore by jamming the hat on her head and putting her camera away in its case. She could never again trust herself to be alone with Zackery Quinn. In those moments of revelation, he had unleashed her sensuality, had brought her alive in a very real, very painful way—and he knew it!

With unhurried movements he gathered the remnants of their lunch and stashed everything in the saddlebag, as if what had happened between them meant nothing to him. Which, of course, it didn't. Only in Alex's imagination had he been as hungry and as desperate with need as she.

How foolish of her to forget even for one second that he held women in contempt. In countless ways he'd let her know that the happiness of his childhood memories had been supplanted by pain. Clearly women served little purpose for him, except to relieve the frustrations no doubt brought on by a failed relationship. Then, any consenting female would do.

Unfortunately for Alex, the experience had flung her headlong into uncharted waters. She fought to regain her composure. Grimly she mounted Gum Drop, prepared to ride as hard and as fast as she could out of Zackery Quinn's life.

"You're right about the roses," he said in a conversational tone a few minutes later, breaking the tension-filled silence as he waited for her to draw even with him. They had left the forest and were headed toward the stable, which according to Alex's calculations had to be at least another hour away. "In a week's time they'll have started to wither."

He eyed her speculatively, making her already chaotic nerves jump like live wires. "Tomorrow I have commitments I can't get out of, but the following day I'm free. Can you arrange your schedule to photograph Domino on Tuesday?"

His question hung in the air, tempting her as surely as Satan had beguiled Eve. She still couldn't account for his sudden entry into her life, but felt she was getting closer to the truth. "What time did you have in mind?"

If he was surprised at her swift capitulation, he didn't show it. "I'll give you a break and come by at eight."

"That will be fine," she said in a deceptively controlled voice before urging Gum Drop forward. The lively mare obviously knew the way home, and she broke into a full gallop, eager to get back to the stable. No more eager than Alex, however.

She sensed that Zackery Quinn wasn't far behind, but she didn't wait for him. If he chose, he could catch up easily. But now that he'd wrung the desired response from her, the chase no longer interested him. What did he *really* want?

More puzzled than ever, Alex decided two could play this game. Come Tuesday, Troy would be the one accompanying him on the shoot. Alex had no intention of being on the premises when he arrived. She would never place herself in such a vulnerable position again.

As soon as she got home, she'd develop the film and study the proofs with Troy, explaining her ideas to him. By Tuesday he should be ready to get a perfect picture of Domino in that magic setting.

And Troy shouldn't have any problem getting there. She'd noticed a dirt track running along the edge of the forest. He could be transported that far by truck. If Zack Quinn carried all the equipment, Troy would be able to make it through the forest on foot, using his crutches.

Her brother was going to be in for a shock!

She'd purposely kept him in the dark about the Circle Q and its owner, because she'd wanted to do some investigating first. Heavens, Troy would go absolutely crazy over the plane ride, let alone the splendor of the ranch. And he'd be in complete awe of Zackery Quinn.

Who wouldn't? Alex moaned to herself. He was the ideal of the American male, a man who reflected the independence and adventure of his ancestors, a man born to be in charge. A Westerner whose land was his life. And he was the man who'd captured Alex's imagination—and her heart.

The one man she could never hope to have.

The sooner she left his kingdom, the sooner she could get back to her ordinary world, to the life she was destined to live, the life she'd always been content to live. *Until now...*

"THAT'S THE LAST of 'em, boss. Good thing, too. You've kept us hoppin'. We're all 'bout ready to collapse—and you don't even seem tired. What's goin' on?" Dusty spoke with the easy camaraderie formed by years of working together, day in, day out.

"You'd be surprised," Zack muttered, leaning against a post to wipe the sweat off his forehead with the back of his arm. It was getting dark outside. They'd been branding for almost fifteen hours. Zack was so consumed with ambivalent thoughts of Alexandria Duncan he could have kept up his frantic pace indefinitely, but the men were obviously exhausted and hungry.

"Tell the guys there'll be a bonus in their next paycheck, Dusty. They did a good job."

"That'll make 'em happy, *if* they survive until then." Dusty chuckled at his own joke and clapped Zack on the shoulder. "Somebody's sure put a burr under your saddle, boss. Take it easy, will ya? Nothin' and no one's worth killin' yourself for. See you in the morning."

"Thanks for the advice, Dusty. I'll think about it."

Soon Zack was alone with only the smell of the branding and the lowing of cattle—the tangible evidence of a life he could always rely on. The land was everything, he'd heard his father say repeatedly. More and more Zack understood what he'd meant.

Shrugging off his pensive mood, he mounted his horse and headed back to the ranch house. It wasn't until he'd grabbed a quick bite to eat and spent a half hour with Randy while they read the newspaper to his father that fatigue set in. After that, he picked up the day's mail and went to his suite.

Once there, he took off his boots and lounged shirtless on the love seat, his head propped up by a couple of pillows. He leafed through the accumulation of correspondence—not a word of which penetrated his consciousness.

He had to face the fact that no matter how hard he'd tried, he couldn't exorcize Alexandria Duncan from his thoughts.

Acting on a compulsion over which he seemed to have no control, he reached inside the nearby box of posters. He pulled one out at random—the picture of her brushing her hair. It didn't do the color of her hair justice. In sunlight, golden strands gleamed among the red. He loved the feel of its weight in his hands.

The memory of that moment the day before, when she'd stopped struggling and he felt her arching warmth, the way her generous mouth gave him kiss for kiss, had almost sent him into shock. He'd had to restrain himself from lowering her to the blanket and making love to her. It was all he'd been able to think about.

He pulled out another picture—Alexandria washing the car—and too late realized his mistake in keeping the photos in his room. Looking at those long legs brought back memories of her body fused to his. He could still smell the flowery scent of her hair dancing about her shoulders. Worst of all, he could imagine her on Domino, the roses her only adornment.... Muttering an oath of self-disgust, he crumpled the poster in his fist and tossed it across the room.

The ringing of the phone brought him to his feet and he hurried to pick up the receiver. Bud was supposed to get back to him with any information he could find on Ms. Duncan's nocturnal activities—if she'd been employed, or was currently employed, by any clubs or hotels in the Tahoe area.

He prayed Bud had uncovered something so unsavory the fire would be doused. Permanently. Otherwise, Zack knew, he was in deep trouble.

He expelled a pent-up breath when he heard Bud's voice. "I know you've been waiting," his friend said. "Based on the pictures you gave me, the good news for Andrew is that no one I've talked to has ever seen or heard of Alexandria Duncan, let alone hired her. But they'd like to," he added, which only increased Zack's turmoil.

"My hunch is, the woman's working her own little game, using her brother. How involved that game is, I don't know. You spent the day with her. What did you find out?"

Too much about his own obsession, he thought, and not a damn thing about her. Nothing he could use as hard evidence.

She'd been adamant in her refusal to pose for him. The only thing that struck him as odd was the way she'd reacted—more like someone who was completely outraged at the very thought of it, as if she'd been injured by the mere suggestion. Which didn't ring true in light of those posters.

"So? What did you find out?" Bud repeated.

Zack's mouth thinned. "Enough to agree with you, Bud. In the beginning, I thought someone else had masterminded the scheme, using her as the bait. But putting together what I've learned from you and Randy, plus observing her at close range—" he said this a touch too harshly "—I no longer believe that.

"But I do think she somehow found out that Randy is Andrew's son. I think there's a distinct possibility she wants to get my nephew in so deep she can embarrass Andrew. Ultimately I believe she'll use blackmail to extort money from him."

"It looks that way," Bud concurred. "For what it's worth," Bud inserted, "psychological studies tend to show that the Polly Perfects of this world, who never rebel or step out of character, often suffer a breakdown of some kind. They go off the deep end one way or another.

"The death of her parents and all that responsibility with no money coming in probably triggered it. I have to admit she's done a hell of a job covering it up, though. That's what makes a case like this so challenging."

Bud, you don't know the half of it.

"Your scenario fits," Zack muttered. "It appears that after figuring out how to exploit her ... assets to their greatest advantage, she pulled up stakes and moved to Reno, instead of a city like Sacramento." She'd admitted to loving the Tahoe area. Little wonder ...

"Right. It's the perfect place to carry on her, uh, line of work."

"A complete break from her former life. A place where no one knows her." Zack warmed to his subject. "A new state that allows gambling and strip shows and wouldn't blink an eye at her operation. No state income tax. In full charge of her brother with no other family members to monitor her activities. Manipulating him without his being aware. Yeah, it all fits."

"Yup. But, Zack, you can't blame the poor kid for his sister's actions. After all, he's still a minor and he probably hasn't got a clue that they could be in serious trouble."

Pouncing on that angle, Zack said, "Yes, her brother is the key to exposing her, and I know exactly how I'm going to do it."

He thanked Bud and they said goodbye, then Zack hung the phone up thoughtfully. It looked as if Troy Duncan had been telling Randy the truth as he knew it. Now to let Randy in on his plan.

Tomorrow morning Zack intended to be at the Write Set-Up by seven rather than eight. The element of surprise would throw her off balance. If she was like most women, she wouldn't be ready for him, which would give him an opportunity to talk to her brother in private.

Zack intended to win the boy over in a way that guaranteed his full cooperation. Whatever it took, Troy would be accompanying them back to the ranch. Zack would get Randy to befriend him—without revealing that Randy Cordell was Jerry Spaulding. If things worked out as Zack envisioned, it was only a matter of time before the treacherous Ms. Duncan was brought to her knees.

CHAPTER FIVE

"HERE ARE THE PROOFS," Alex announced as she entered the kitchen. "Let's see what you think of them." She spread them out on the table where Troy was eating a midnight snack.

She'd had no opportunity until now to sit down with her brother. On her return from the Circle Q, she'd found the house empty. Troy had left a note indicating he was sleeping over at his friend Bruce's place in Grass Valley and would be home the next day.

At least it meant he hadn't moped around the house all day. She wanted him to have fun and not lose contact with his buddies.

But when the next day arrived and he still wasn't home by ten in the evening, she grew alarmed and reached for the phone to start making a few calls. That was when she heard the front door open and close, and he hobbled into the kitchen, whistling.

By the sparkle in his eyes she could tell he'd had a great time. And because she needed his cooperation as never before, she refrained from chastising him for being so inconsiderate and fixed him a meal, instead. Her tactics paid off, and they enjoyed a camaraderie that had been missing the past couple of months.

"Wow!" he exclaimed, examining one proof after the other. "This dude's spread is fantastic." His intense blue eyes fastened on her face. "What's the name of it again?"

"The Circle Q." Alex paused. "It's probably the best-known ranch in the state, Troy."

"Did you have any idea when you agreed to photograph Mr. Quinn's property that he was the owner of all this?"

"Yes," she said in a quiet voice as she leaned over his shoulder. Troy's reaction to the proofs was everything she'd anticipated and more.

He shook his head in awe. "Can you imagine the kind of money a ranch the size of the Circle Q must haul in?"

Actually she couldn't. Clearing her throat, she said, "Mr. Quinn wants Domino photographed in this setting." She pointed to the proof showing the roses in the forest.

As Troy finished off his pizza and bent his head in concentration, she added, "I thought it would make an interesting shot if the horse stood under the spray so it looked like he was wearing the winner's garland at the Kentucky Derby."

"Yeah," he murmured, "but check out those white birch trees on the right and the dapple effect from the sun. See all those interesting lights and shadows? A white stallion emerging between their trunks would be more dramatic and play up his coloring. We could try a couple of shots with and without a cluster of roses in one corner to see what works best. What do you think?"

The minute the words came out of his mouth, she knew he was right. She placed her hands gently on his shoulders. "You've proven once again that you're the true photographer in this family. Mr. Quinn won't be sorry he came to us." *Even if he did approach me with a completely different reason in mind.*

She'd never been so confused in her life. She could still feel the warmth and pressure of Zack's body, still taste his mouth against her own. Tomorrow would be too soon to see him again. She couldn't face him, not when all she could think about, all she craved, was to be in his arms—to finish what they'd started in the forest.

"I hope he's not coming at five-thirty," Troy moaned.

She picked up his empty plate and glass and walked to the sink. "You're in luck," she called over her shoulder. "He'll be by for you at eight."

"Me?" he asked, perplexed. "You're the one who went out and did all the preliminary work."

Heat suffused her face. Thank heavens Troy would never know what had really happened!

Sucking in her breath, Alex turned around, resting her hip against the counter. "If you could have ridden on a horse, you would have been the one to go yesterday. Fortunately this favorite spot of his is accessible by truck. You'll only have to use your crutches to walk a little way in."

She paused before saying, "This could be your big break, Troy. If he likes your work, you'll be paid more money than you've ever made before. And I'm sure he'll recommend you to his friends locally and around the country. Who knows—your dream to be a roving free-lance photographer might come true sooner than you think!''

Others touted Troy's athleticism, but Alex knew the importance of his artistic gift. She knew his curiosity and sense of adventure would make him want to slip the bonds of home and find out what the world had to offer. He wasn't anything like their mother and father who'd been content to stay at home. After their death, she'd promised herself she'd help Troy realize his dream, no matter how great the sacrifice.

After the injury to her brother's leg, Zackery Quinn's unexpected entry into their lives was a mixed blessing. She wouldn't let anything go wrong now, not when it could be the turning point for Troy.

The scraping of his chair against the linoleum broke her reverie. Troy had gotten up from the table and was reaching for his crutches. He made his way toward her, excitement illuminating his face. ''Exactly how much did he offer to pay you for this photo session?''

''He hasn't mentioned a figure yet. A man with his kind of money never does. It'll all depend on the finished product.'' She flashed him a brilliant smile. ''Because you're the one shooting the pictures, I'm sure it'll be a generous amount.''

He looked taken back. ''You really mean that, don't you?''

''Of course. I've always believed in your talent, Troy. You're a lot better than Dad ever was, and that's saying a great deal.''

An odd expression she couldn't decipher clouded his eyes. Then he threw one arm around her neck and hugged her tight. "Thanks." The simple reply spoke volumes. Maybe everything was going to be okay.

When he released her she averted her eyes and hurried over to the table to gather the proofs. "As long as you're going to be gone all day tomorrow, I've decided to drive to Marysville and spend the day with Sally. She's been begging me to come ever since we moved here, so I think I'll take off around six-thirty in the morning. That way I'll have plenty of time to stop in Grass Valley, say hello to a couple of friends and close out that one checking account."

And avoid having to explain to Zackery Quinn why I won't be accompanying Troy to the ranch.

Putting the proofs in an envelope, she turned to her brother and handed it to him. "We both deserve a holiday, don't you think?"

"Yeah," he murmured, but there was still a faintly troubled expression on his face she didn't understand. "Uh, who are you going to visit in Grass Valley?"

"Oh, I'll probably drop in on Vicky and see how big her baby has grown," she speculated. "Why?"

"No reason." He shrugged, then smiled wryly. "I guess I'm picking up a few bad habits from you. Maybe you don't realize it, but I worry about you, too."

Alex blinked. "May I quote you on that?"

Troy broke into good-natured laughter and had the grace to blush. "I'm gonna hit the sack. See you tomorrow night, Alex. Say hi to Sally for me."

"I will," she murmured. "And I don't need to tell you to have a good time tomorrow with Mr. Quinn.

You're in for the thrill of your life. Wait till you see the view of the ranch from his plane!''

WELL BEFORE SIX the following morning, Alex was lying awake, reliving those moments in Zackery Quinn's arms. When she couldn't stand it any longer, she got up and did some work in her office before leaving for the day. On her way out, she assembled the equipment Troy would need for the shoot and left it by the front door.

As she sped along the familiar highway, it dawned on her that she hadn't even called Sally to make sure she was home, let alone find out if it would be a convenient time for a visit. Alex didn't want to impose on her best friend, who'd been married less than a year. Russ taught shop at the local high school; he'd been the one to interest Troy in ham radio, bringing the boy out of his severest depression. Alex appreciated Russ's generosity and didn't want to be a nuisance if he and Sally had other plans, especially now that school was out.

When she reached Grass Valley, Alex stopped at a pay phone to call Sally, who lived in the nearby town of Marysville. No one answered, so she called Sally's parents and found out that her friend and Russ had left for Yosemite the week before.

Although she'd been looking forward to seeing Sally, Alex didn't mind. The important thing was that by now Troy would be strapped into the cockpit, exclaiming over everything he saw and silently worshiping the man at the controls. Her brother would be in awe of Zackery Quinn, with his aura of command and his exciting, larger-than-life presence.

She rested her head against the glass of the phone booth before hanging up. *How was she ever going to forget him?*

Furious with herself for wanting something so far out of reach, she got back into her car and drove to her favorite café for breakfast. She chatted with the owners for an hour or so. The couple had been good friends of her parents and wanted a rundown of everything that had been happening to her and Troy.

Afterward she called her friend Vicky, who sounded delighted to hear from Alex. She invited her over immediately, since she was home with her four-month-old son.

A short while later, cuddling Vicky's baby son and giving him his bottle, Alex was tormented even more by thoughts of Zack. She imagined holding her own baby in her arms. She pictured a robust child with dark brown hair and eyes, reminiscent of his father's. . . .

After an hour or so with Vicky, she felt too restless to impose herself on her friend any longer. Alex left, promising to call soon, and headed for the bank. On impulse she stopped by Bruce Hutchinson's home. She wanted to thank him and his parents for Troy's outing. It had certainly done her brother a world of good.

But when she turned into the driveway, Bruce's mother, who'd been working in her garden, hurried up to the car. She immediately began commiserating over Troy's broken leg, which had prevented him from joining Bruce and his other old friends on the camp-out they'd gone on to celebrate the end of school. The whole group of them had apparently gotten on the phone the week before, begging Troy to go along. But when Troy said the doctor still wouldn't give his permission, they went without him Friday night and weren't expected to return until Thursday evening.

Alex hid her shock at the news and chatted with Bruce's mother for a few more minutes before starting the car. She was halfway back to Reno before it registered that she'd forgotten to stop at the bank. But the instant she'd learned that Troy had blatantly lied to her about his whereabouts over a twenty-four-hour period, everything else had fled her mind.

Suddenly the odd expression on Troy's face and his question about whom she'd be visiting in Grass Valley began to make sense. Tears sprang to her eyes. It seemed painfully ironic that last night she'd believed she and Troy had reached a new understanding.

By the time she pulled into the driveway, she felt as if her whole world had been turned upside down and there was no way to right it.

Work. She would concentrate on work until Troy returned from the ranch. Then she'd get to the bottom of his lies. She dreaded the inevitable confrontation, but until she had some answers, she'd never be able to trust him again. And that wasn't the way she wanted to live her life. Zackery Quinn's advent into her troubled existence only exacerbated a situation fast spiraling out of control.

As soon as she entered the office, Alex picked up the phone, heard the clicking noise that indicated messages, and punched in the number to listen to them.

She loved the phone company's new answering-machine service. The caller could leave as long a message as he or she wanted, which was good for her business.

But she almost dropped the receiver when the last message began and she heard Troy's voice. He sounded more excited than she'd ever heard him.

"Alex, it's me! I'm calling from the Circle Q ranch house. Wow, you oughtta see this place! Anyway, while we were out taking pictures, Zack's nephew came to get us because Zack's father had another stroke. The nurse doesn't think it was serious enough to put him in the hospital though. He lives with Zack, and he's been sick for a long time.

"So, Zack rushed off with Randy and sent Pete and a couple of other guys to help with Domino and to take me and my equipment back to the ranch house. But what I'm really calling about, Alex, is that Zack offered me a job on his ranch for the summer! I'll make more money than I could make in a whole year in Reno, and I'd live here. He said there are dozens of things I can do, even with my bad leg. He told me to say you're free to come out here any time this summer and stay as long as you want. Isn't that *fantastic?*"

As he rattled on joyously, Alex felt an adrenaline rush that made her cheeks go hot. "His nephew, who's my age, is staying with him right now while his dad's away. And get this—his name's Randy Cordell! And guess who his father is? *Andrew Cordell, the governor of Nevada!* Randy's mother was Zack's sister, but she died. He's so cool you wouldn't believe it. And

Alex—they both invited me to stay over for a few days to think about it.''

Alex frowned. It didn't come as any great shock to realize that some of the biggest nongambling money in the state was linked to the governorship, but it did surprise her. Now that she thought about it, she did remember hearing about the premature death of the governor's wife. As Alex recalled, the first lady had been a charming brunette. She must have been Zackery Quinn's sister!

Alex had never heard her brother sound so elated. She'd known that meeting Zack Quinn would be an unforgettable experience for him, but she'd never expected all this to result from a morning's shoot.

How could Troy be on a first-name basis with everyone on the Quinn ranch, including the owner and his nephew, so fast? What was going on? Zackery Quinn was up to something. She felt it in her bones.

For some inexplicable reason, some reason known only to himself, he'd hired them to take pictures. Now he was interfering in their personal lives. He had absolutely no business making this kind of offer to her brother. Especially now, with Troy feeling so vulnerable and missing his father so desperately.

She didn't believe for one second that Zackery Quinn had hired Troy for altruistic reasons, and the fact that he'd done all this without consulting her first made her livid.

Even though the trip to Grass Valley had revealed some unpleasant truths, Alex now regretted her decision not to travel to the ranch with Troy. In her absence, Zackery Quinn had won Troy's admiration as easily as he'd stolen Alex's heart.

She listened impatiently to the rest of her brother's message. "Since I don't want to put him out while he's still worried about his father, I'll just plan to stay here with Randy and get busy."

Oh, no, you won't, Alex vowed. Aside from every other consideration, Zackery Quinn's father was ill, and he didn't need any more complications at a time like that.

"Yolanda's going to feed us in a few minutes, and then Jocco, his field foreman, and Randy are going to show me the ropes. That's why I'm calling. I didn't want you to be worried when you got back from Marysville and I still hadn't shown up. When things quiet down in a day or two he'll fly me back to Reno and I'll develop the film. I got some great shots. Pete told me his stallion's worth over a million bucks. Alex, I think I just died and went to heaven!"

Alex groaned.

"Oh, one more thing I thought you'd like to know—" Troy had lowered his voice "—Zack Quinn is Nevada's most eligible bachelor. According to Randy, every woman around, married or not, would like to get hitched to him, but he's not having any of it because of some woman who hurt him bad."

Alex's heart turned over. So it *had* been a love affair that had embittered him. As Alex had learned from personal experience, he could get anything he wanted from a woman without committing himself to marriage.

"Stick with me and you could have an inside shot," Troy finished. "Talk to you soon."

They'd talk soon, all right! She slammed down the receiver with so much force papers flew everywhere. Grabbing her purse, she locked the front door and ran to her car, estimating it would probably take a couple of hours to reach the Circle Q.

Before the day was over she'd snatch her brother away from Zackery Quinn and drag him back home. Then she'd go after Mr. Quinn and demand a full explanation!

A GENTLE TAP on the open door brought Zack's head around. Yolanda signaled for him to join her in the hall. With a nod, the nurse indicated that there was no need for him to stay in his father's room.

"Would you go and tell Yolanda I'll be out in a minute, Noreen?" he murmured. "Why don't you take a break while you're at it?"

"All right."

As soon as he was alone with his father, Zack leaned over the frail old man and grasped his hand. "Dad? I don't know how much you can hear, or if you know what's going on," he said in a choked whisper. "But I'm here, and I love you."

He wiped his eyes with his other hand. "I pray you're not in pain. Everyone here needs you, Dad, but I imagine by now you're ready to join Mom. Don't worry about the Circle Q. I'll take care of everything as long as there's breath in my body. And Randy is starting to love the place, too, so be assured all is well." He cleared his throat. "I have to go for a little while, but I'll be back. I know you like Noreen. She's with you night and day when I can't be. I'll see you soon.''

Zack straightened and released his father's warm but limp hand. Everything possible had been done for him. The latest stroke had caused the left side of his mouth to sag a little, but other than that, he seemed no different. According to the physician Zack had talked to earlier in the day, his father's heart was still pretty strong. He could go on like this for an indeterminate period.

Dropping a light kiss on his father's pale forehead, Zack left the bedroom and Noreen slipped back inside. He went down the hall in search of Yolanda.

''I'm sorry I bothered you,'' she said, ''but I thought you'd want to know. Troy's sister, Ms. Duncan, arrived a few minutes ago wanting to pick up her brother.''

The mention of Troy's sister wrested Zack away from his worry about his father. He'd known it was only a matter of time before Ms. Duncan showed up, but he hadn't counted on her driving to the ranch tonight. According to Troy, his sister had decided to spend the day in Marysville with a friend and had already done a considerable amount of driving.

She's worried.

Nothing could have pleased Zack more. Apparently Troy's phone call to his sister had thrown a wrench into her plans for the summer. Without his cooperation in taking photographs and finding new ''customers'' over ham radio, she'd have to revamp her whole undercover business.

"I'll take care of her, Yolanda."

"That's just the problem, Zack. She's gone."

His satisfied smile quickly faded. "What do you mean, gone?"

"When I told her Troy was out in the truck with Randy and Jocco and might not be back till real late, she acted upset and said she'd drive to Yerington and wait for a while, then call again to see if he'd returned."

On a swift intake of breath he said, "Why didn't you stop her?"

"I didn't have a choice." She lifted her shoulders expressively. "I told her to wait in the living room while I went to get you, but she told me not to disturb you. Said you had enough on your mind with your father. Then she hurried out of the house and drove off."

"That's all right, Yolanda. I'll catch up with her." He spoke with a ferocity that made his housekeeper dart him an incredulous look.

In a few quick strides he reached a side door that gave him access to the back of the house and the garage where he kept his Range Rover. Pulling the keys from the visor, he started the engine and barreled past the house and down the drive, determined to head her off before she decided to go back to Reno.

Every time he thought he had her figured out, she did something unpredictable. Like not even being there when he arrived at her house early that morning. Even now, the shock of her unexpected disappearance made his hands tighten on the steering wheel, turning the knuckles white. He'd been counting the hours until he saw her again, eager to continue play-ing her until he was ready to reel her in.

And then there was her brother. To Zack's sur-prise, Troy was one of the most mature, talented and intelligent teenagers he'd ever met. He hadn't been prepared to like the boy, not after hearing him gloat over the success of their illegal mail-order business with Randy.

Troy was obviously a natural athlete, yet he made light of his broken leg, handling himself and his crutches with a dexterity Zack could only admire. The boy displayed impeccable manners and genuine charm. If there was anything to criticize, it was his unmistakable resemblance to his sister. He, too, had been given more than his fair share of good looks.

Unlike Randy, Troy wouldn't feel the need for an expensive car to impress a girl. With his attractive personality, he'd have no problem in that depart-ment—just like his amoral redheaded sister.

Gritting his teeth, Zack pressed the accelerator to the floor, whizzing past a car pulled to the side of the road in an alkali bed. Because of the growing dark-ness, it took a few seconds for him to register the fact that it was a green Honda. He'd seen a green Honda parked in the drive beside the Duncan house.

Well, well, he muttered to himself and made a U-turn, gratified that she'd saved him the trouble of hunting for her in town. He drove back to a spot across the road from the car and got out. She refused to look at him.

At first he thought she was playing games, until he tapped on her window and she turned her head nervously in his direction. He saw a flash of fear in her eyes before she realized who it was, and right that second, she looked so vulnerable and so damn beautiful Zack had a hard time believing she could exploit her brother and do all the things he knew she did. But her expression quickly changed to something approaching anger as she rolled down the window, obviously furious that he'd caught up with her at all.

"An isolated country road isn't the best place for a woman to park, Ms. Duncan. Especially at night. Unless—" he paused insolently "—you have a good reason."

He couldn't help noticing the way her chest heaved in indignation. In fact, he couldn't help staring at her—her flushed face, her slender hands as they clenched the steering wheel. And her hair, as attractively disheveled as it had been the day his hands had wandered through it while they kissed. Much to his disgust, that was exactly what he wanted to do right now.

She averted her eyes. "My car overheated. There must be a leak in the radiator or something. I'm waiting for it to cool down."

"That could take some time," he said dispassionately, noting the tremor that ran through her body. "Long enough to get you into the kind of trouble I don't think even *you* would be prepared for."

Her head reared back at the remark, causing her hair to swirl around one shoulder. "Are you always so charming, Mr. Quinn, or is it something about me in particular, that brings out your chivalrous streak?"

Her sarcasm wasn't wasted on him, nor the angry sparks flashing from those jewel-tone eyes.

Without asking her permission, he reached inside and unlocked the door, intentionally brushing against the softness of her forearm. She was still trembling. He couldn't account for it, unless she knew her game was up. "Would you prefer I left you to your own devices?" he asked dryly, opening the door. "I can't guarantee that the next male, or group of males, won't stop and decide to *help* you, whether you want their form of help or not."

Her dilemma amused him. Under the circumstances, which of the two evils would she consider the most tolerable?

CHAPTER SIX

ASSUMING THAT CLOAK of dignity she wore so well on occasion, Alexandria Duncan swung her legs around, affording him a glimpse of enticing ankles and calves beneath the hem of her summery print dress.

He would have helped her from the car, but she insisted on doing it by herself, making certain she rolled up the window and locked the door before heading across the road. For a brief moment, the mesmerizing movement of her lovely body drove every other thought from his mind.

Drawing on what little self-control he had left, he opened the passenger door and helped her into his Range Rover. He seated himself and turned on the ignition, then said, "When we get home I'll send a couple of men to tow your car back to the house."

She finally deigned to look at him through those long silky lashes, smoothing a few wayward strands of hair from her flushed cheek. "Look, Mr. Quinn. I must admit I'm thankful you came along when you did, but I'd prefer to be driven into Yerington. You can leave me there and I'll arrange with a garage to get my car towed and repaired. Naturally I'll pay you for your time and the gas."

He didn't respond right away. "There's no gas station open within miles of here, and in any event they wouldn't send out a tow truck before tomorrow afternoon at the earliest. In that length of time anything could happen to your car."

With a frustrated sigh, she buried her face in her hands. "I'm sorry." After a moment she lifted her head. "I had no idea this would happen. I hate disturbing you when your father had a stroke today. That's the reason I drove to the ranch in the first place—to get Troy and take him home so you wouldn't have to worry about him on top of everything else."

She'd told Yolanda the same thing. Her show of concern would fool anyone who didn't know the real reason she wanted her brother off the ranch.

"Perhaps Troy failed to tell you that my father's stroke was less serious than first presumed and he's sleeping as comfortably as usual."

"Nevertheless, you must be worried. From what I understand you already have a nephew staying with you. This isn't the time to be dealing with an uninvited guest."

"You're wrong," he asserted as he drove off down the road toward the ranch, intrigued that she would carry her act this far. "Didn't your brother explain that I've put him on the payroll?"

She nodded and he could just make out the line of her profile. "He mentioned something about working for you this summer. It was generous of you to offer, but I'm afraid the question of his employment is a matter for Troy and me to discuss in private before any kind of decision can be made."

Zack admired her ability to contain herself when she was obviously bristling with anger. "He thought the news would please you," he murmured, watching her to determine the effect of his words. "He told me you were upset when he turned down the job offer from the man who owns the auto-parts shop."

"I wasn't..." she began. "Yes, I was upset," she amended. "At first. But it's Troy's life and I want him to be happy with the job he chooses. H-he's been depressed since his leg injury." Her voice shook with so much emotion Zack wondered if anyone could fake that kind of response.

"Would it relieve your mind to know he didn't hesitate one second when I suggested hiring him?"

"Oh, that I can believe." She let out a defeated little sigh. "That was clear from the message he left on our answering machine. He's at a very impressionable age, you know. He's feeling displaced because of our recent move from California, he's still grieving for Mom and Dad, and he's badly in need of a male role model. A few hours on the Circle Q and he's smitten. It's hardly a surprise. The way he's feeling right now, he'd probably jump off a cliff blindfolded if you asked him to."

Zack's lips quirked in amusement. "I wouldn't expect that of him right away. At least not until his cast's off."

Her delightful ripple of laughter came as a shock, almost making him forget the trap he'd laid to ensnare her. She turned her head toward him. "Why did you offer Troy a job? The truth, now." The hint of pleading in her voice disturbed him in ways he didn't want to analyze. He didn't answer immediately.

"Troy's a straightforward young man with lofty goals and the intelligence to attain them," he finally began. "I admire those qualities in anyone, but more particularly in your brother, because he's also handling the loss of his parents. Not only that, he's come to grips with the fact that he'll never play football again and isn't crying about it. For those reasons alone, I'd like to do whatever I can to help nurture his potential. There's no telling what he'll accomplish one day—*if* he isn't held back."

Even in the shadowy interior, he thought her face lost color. "What do you mean?"

"I don't know. Maybe you should tell me. It's obvious he feels—" Zack paused, as if trying to choose his words carefully "—stifled at home."

"Stifled?" she whispered, her voice full of pain. It was the last reaction he expected from her. "Did he actually tell you that?"

"Of course not. It's what I read between the lines. He talked a lot about all the sacrifices you've made, the way you've put your own life on hold to give him everything he wants. He loves you, but he's suffering from guilt because he can't handle all your...expectations."

"I only want what's best for Troy," she said vehemently. "I'd do anything for him!"

"Except give him his freedom?" Zack noted the stricken look on her face. "If you let him go, one day he'll thank you for it. Right now, the only way he can see to throw off that guilt is to become independent and make his own decisions by cutting the apron strings.'' And to escape the power she had over him, he added silently.

"I need to talk to Troy," she said in a no-nonsense tone. "How much longer do you think it'll be before he gets back from his ride with your nephew?"

Zack pulled the Range Rover to a stop in front of the ranch house. He leaned back in the seat to face her, fighting to prevent a smile from forming. "I'm afraid not until morning."

"What?"

Her cry of enraged disbelief told him he'd hit a nerve. "When Troy said he wanted to see more of the ranch, Jocco offered to drive him and Randy out on the range to experience a night under the stars with some of the stockmen. Figuring how you'd react after everything he'd confided to me, I suggested he obtain your permission first. But he said you'd probably get home too late for that. He also said he didn't think you'd begrudge him the opportunity."

"But you could have stopped your foreman from introducing the idea in the first place," she fired back.

Zack shrugged. "If your brother works for me, Jocco will be his immediate boss," he reasoned calmly. "And though I may have offered him a job, it's not signed, sealed and delivered until he sees all aspects of ranch life and knows what he's getting into. That's why Jocco took time out of his busy schedule to accommodate your brother. Naturally, nothing will be decided until you and Troy come to some sort of agreement."

"Naturally," came her icy rejoinder. "And you've made certain he'll spend the most wonderful night of his life in the wide open spaces," she said mockingly, "so there's no way I can look like anything but a mean interfering witch if I don't give my approval for him to work at the Circle Q."

One dark brow lifted. "A little while ago you said you'd do anything for him. If he tells you tomorrow that he'd like to work for me, then I presume we'll see how sincere you are."

Anger radiated from her. "Put it any way you like, Mr. Quinn. You've taken unfair psychological advantage of a minor."

"And what do we call what you've done to your own brother, Ms. Duncan?" he asked brutally.

"What goes on between me and Troy is absolutely none of your business."

His expression hardened. "That's true, as long as it doesn't hurt anyone else."

"Hurt anyone else?" she repeated, then threw back her head, eyes blazing. "Ah, so we're getting to the truth at last. I've heard nothing but cryptic remarks and innuendo since the great cattle king decided to fly from his lofty heights and grace a mere mortal's establishment with his presence. Do you really think I bought your lame excuse for coming to the Write Set-Up?"

He grinned wickedly. "You're on Circle Q property right now, so it seems you did."

"Because I knew you had ulterior motives!"

"And you went along with me, anyway," he pointed out, enjoying her discomfiture. At last she was revealing her true character.

"Of course!" she snapped. "I was curious to discover the real reason you commissioned a relatively unknown little business to do an ad for you."

"You know what they say about curiosity."

"And you know what they say about a wolf in sheep's clothing," she returned. "All right. You've had your fun. You've dangled your carrot in front of Troy and you've got him hooked. You've sunk your teeth into me where you knew it would hurt the most. And now I'm here alone, completely at your mercy. That's what you wanted.

"Now have the decency to tell me *why* you've gone to these elaborate lengths. If Troy or I have done something to injure you in some way—though I can't imagine what, since neither of us had ever seen you until you walked through our shop door the other day—then tell me. Say what you have to say, and we'll apologize and try to make amends. If that's possible," she added with remarkable hauteur.

"You admitted seeing me at the horse show a year ago, or doesn't that count?" he muttered gravely.

After a tension-filled pause she said, "That's true. So I lied. You can add it to my list of sins, whatever they are."

Zack stared hard at her, taken aback by the way she'd recovered her composure. She really had no conscience. What a fool he was for not learning his lesson the first time! He supposed that in some secret part of his psyche, he'd hoped for a different outcome, and he was surprised at the sharp disappointment he felt. This went far beyond the damaged male pride of an innocent twenty-year-old.

"I make it a policy never to discuss business until my guest is comfortable. Since you'll be spending the night at the Circle Q and we've both had a long day, I suggest we retire to the house, where Yolanda will show you to your room. You can freshen up, have some dinner. Just tell her what you'd like and she'll prepare it for you.

"After I've looked in on my father, I'll meet you in my study. Shall we say half an hour? A woman like you doesn't need time to make herself presentable. You're perfect just the way you are." He smiled, but the light didn't reach his eyes. "But of course you already know that, don't you?"

"Ms. DUNCAN? Yolanda thought you might change your mind about eating, so she asked me to bring you this salad in case you're hungry." A dark-haired maid with a friendly smile slipped into the guest bedroom and placed a tray on an octagonal table near the huge picture window.

"Thank you," she murmured to the girl, who hurried back out. Alex was too bemused by her sumptuous surroundings to manage a conversation. More than that, she was dreading the confrontation with Zackery Quinn. Her apprehension had been growing since the moment he'd found her sitting in her car by the side of the road, waiting for the needle on the temperature gauge to drop.

Of all the times for her car to act up! She'd purposely gone to Yerington to avoid seeing him. And now here she was, his prisoner in a jeweled cage.

Alex headed for the table. The room was spacious, carpeted in a luscious melon color, with off-white wicker furniture and plump printed pillows. She observed her surroundings with detachment. It was a lovely room, comfortable, airy and undeniably feminine.

With her stomach churning in anxiety, she knew she couldn't eat the salad, but the iced tea looked delicious. While she drank it, she tried to imagine what unforgivable sin she and Troy had committed against the owner of the Circle Q that would cause him to go to all this trouble.

If they'd done something that indirectly affected him in some way, though she couldn't imagine how, why hadn't he said so when he came to her shop that morning? Why the charade?

A glance at her watch indicated her half hour was almost up. Not wanting to prolong the inevitable, she dashed into the adjoining bathroom, where every possible necessity had been provided. She washed her face, brushed her hair and applied a fresh coating of coral lipstick.

Once she felt presentable, she left the guest room, which was located in the west wing on the second story of the sprawling ranch house, and spent a minute or two exploring. She'd been unable to resist running up the stairs to the third story, which rose from the center structure of the early-American style house and had to be at least forty feet from floor to ceiling. She supposed the master of the house had his aerie there. Looking out of his window must be like observing his land from a low-flying aircraft. Finally she went downstairs to the first floor.

There, the main room had twenty-five-foot-high cross-beamed cathedral ceilings. The outer walls were almost completely glassed, and in daylight would provide stunning vistas.

No wonder Troy was in such a state of happiness. The prospect of working in these surroundings would make anything else pale into insignificance. And despite the pain that lay ahead for her, Alex couldn't deny the intensity of her own feelings. Zackery Quinn wasn't like any man she'd ever met. Even his hostility didn't obscure that. But there was no doubt she was about to face a very angry man. Automatically she quickened her steps.

She reached the main entry and gazed in wonder at the huge chandelier. She'd barely glanced at it earlier. Designed with dozens of glowing lamps, it hung suspended from the center beam of the redwood ceiling. The lights were reflected in the coppery-red Mexican floor tiles below.

As Alex followed the housekeeper's directions to the study she spied smaller replicas of the same chandelier hanging in the resort-sized dining and living rooms off to the right.

One whole wall of every hue of rock from black to pink, the kind she'd seen in the Walker River, formed the fireplace. Above the mantel was a portrait of a man she assumed to be the first Zackery Quinn. He overlooked the vast expanse of lawn surrounding the house and the outbuildings in the distance.

Area rugs made by Walker River Indians covered the tile and hardwood floors. She admired them as she made her way along an open corridor lined with old family portraits and scenes of Reno and Carson City in the 1800s.

Had the circumstances been different, Alex could have spent hours looking at the paintings and photographs—especially the photographs portraying a much younger Zackery Quinn, his dashing good looks already in evidence. Alex wished she'd known him then, before he developed that hard veneer of cynicism. Even when his kisses left her aching for more, there'd been a savagery about his lovemaking that wounded her.

Only once in the short time since she'd met him had she caught a glimpse of the man he must have been. But those moments had vanished quickly, and she doubted they could ever be recaptured.

Yolanda had said Alex would find his study at the end of the hall to the right of the living room. She reached two floor-to-ceiling doors with huge antlers above the lintels and knocked, wanting to get this over with as soon as possible. When there was no reply she knocked again, then turned the handle and entered.

If he'd been detained because his father needed him, he'd send someone to tell her, she thought. In the meantime, she'd look at the books on his shelves, which covered one whole wall.

She recognized his stamp everywhere. From the dark oak floors to the leather chairs and couches, from the antique rolltop desk to the photographs of his prized Arabians mounted on the walls, this room shouted his private domain. She wandered over to the trophy case that held dozens of horse-show cups and plaques. What interested her most was the display of photographs. One in particular caught her attention.

Her host couldn't have been more than six. His arm was raised to try to embrace the neck of a Shetland pony, which wore a winner's garland. *His first pony.* She smiled at the memory of the story he'd told her in the desert forest, then studied the ecstatic smile on his young face. He must have been born with a love for animals, because there were other snaps of him romping with a pair of collies.

Curious to see what kind of knickknacks he kept on the highly polished wood mantel, she moved to the stone fireplace and picked up one of the small pictures to examine it closely.

A black-haired man, slightly taller and leaner than Zackery Quinn, stood next to him. Both of their handsome burnished faces grinned into the camera, their eyes glazed as if they'd had a little too much to drink. They were dressed like shepherds and didn't look more than twenty or twenty-one. Rugged mountain peaks—the Swiss Alps?—formed the backdrop.

She picked up other little framed pictures showing the two men mountain-climbing, fishing, partying with friends. One photo depicted her host and his friend on the terrace of a mountain inn, standing with their arms around a black eyed beauty. She reached for it to study the details.

Is this the woman who hurt him so badly?

Alex felt a stab of pain and recognized it as jealousy.

"I like a guest who has no problem making herself at home."

She jumped at the wintry sound of his voice, then quickly restored the picture to its original spot. Refusing to be intimidated, she whirled around to face him. Another mistake.

She studied the sun-darkened face, the arrogant set of his winged brows. Her gaze lowered, following the bold lines of his supple male body. His silk shirt of rich claret, open at the neck, revealed more bronzed skin, with a dusting of hair.

A flood of heat rose through her body to her face. She couldn't sustain his mocking stare. "You said half an hour," she managed to croak. "Since I'm anxious to discover what it is Troy and I have unwittingly done to you, I took you at your word."

He folded his arms, once more drawing her attention to his powerful body, tensed despite his casual gesture. "I think I'm disappointed in you, Ms. Duncan. I intentionally left you alone in my study, expecting that your curiosity would lead you straight to my desk and the damaging evidence."

Alex could hear what he was saying and could tell that he meant every word of it, but she didn't have the faintest idea what he was talking about. "I wouldn't presume to rifle through your private papers, or whatever you keep in your desk," she said in a cool voice. "But since I was summoned here by royal command, I didn't think you'd mind my looking at these photographs...." She shrugged helplessly.

His eyes were dark slits. "You're going to play this to the bitter end, aren't you?"

She'd had enough! "All right! You win!" Tossing her head in defiant Duncan style, she marched toward the desk, her hair flouncing about her face and shoulders in a fiery red cloud. She had no idea what to look for, but his obvious certainty that she was guilty of something left her no choice.

Unless his housekeeper had straightened things, which Alex very much doubted, Mr. Quinn kept his affairs in immaculate order. The only thing lying on top of his desk was a large, stiff brown envelope.

A quick glance told her he was waiting for her to open it. Determined to follow this through, she snatched it up and lifted the flap.

Her father had always said a touch of humor never hurt at a time like this. Flashing her host an impudent smile that made her eyes sizzle wickedly, she grabbed hold of what was inside and pulled it out with a dramatic flair. She had the satisfaction of watching his mouth tauten in suppressed fury.

"And now, ladies and gentlemen, the moment we've all been waiting for. The winner is..."

Her voice faded when she beheld her own face on a fourteen-by-twenty full-color poster. She recognized the expression that greeted her in the mirror every morning while she was still dazed from sleep, trying to get the snarls out of her hair.

Troy!

In shock, she looked at the picture underneath and saw herself in her oldest skimpiest T-shirt soaking wet from washing the Honda, and wearing a pair of cutoffs she'd long since thrown out because by accident she'd made them too short to be worn in public.

Alex hardly dared look at the next poster. When she took a peek, she gasped and a moan lodged in her throat. Unable to bear the thought that Zackery Quinn had seen these, she tore the posters into shreds and deposited them in the wastebasket.

If anything, the gesture highlighted the accusation in his eyes. "I'm still waiting for an answer," he said.

"I'm waiting for it myself!" she exploded, folding her arms to protect herself from his gaze. She felt so shaken by Troy's obvious betrayal she didn't know where to look.

What in heaven's name has been going on in Troy's mind? All the deceit! Was he striking back at the injustice of losing both parents? Or did he hate her so much for being in charge of his life that he decided to play an embarrassing joke on her? Even so, what did any of it have to do with Zackery Quinn?

She raised her head and eyed him levelly. "For the sake of my sanity, would you please tell me why Troy would even show you those awful pictures, let alone get them blown up into posters and leave them in your possession?" She paused to catch her breath. "I'll be the first to agree those photos should never have seen the light of day, but I fail to see how they've injured you. By now it's obvious the humiliation is all mine."

"Humiliation?" he murmured in a dangerous tone. "Come now, Ms. Duncan. You can drop your act of outraged indignation with me. You—better than anyone—know the effect of those photographs on a man."

She didn't misunderstand the insinuation, and it rekindled her anger. "Is this some kind of riddle?" she lashed out, helpless to unravel the mystery.

He drawled insolently, "You demand your pound of flesh, don't you? Well, let's see if I can oblige." While Alex stood there wondering if she was having a nightmare, he reached inside the desk drawer and brought out a stack of folded brochures. He handed her one. "I can keep this up as long as you can." The last was said with a definite smirk.

Feeling the sickness welling in the pit of her stomach, Alex took the heavy-stock paper from his hand, careful not to brush his fingers. The front and back of the brochure had her name, Alexandria, in faultless calligraphy. She recognized Troy's artistic hand and tried to swallow, but her mouth had gone dry and her hands were shaking so hard they wouldn't function.

"Here, let me help," he offered when he saw her difficulty. He opened the brochure for her with a flourish. What she saw almost made her pass out.

Her cry of rage and anguish filled the study. The left side of the brochure showed a dozen posters of Alex in different poses, including the three she'd just torn up, with the words "Love, Alexandria" written across the bottom of each one.

The right side of the brochure invited the buyer to pick any posters from the catalogue and remit the portion below with a twenty-five-dollar check for each order to Steve Bringhurst, 4957 Acorn Drive, Carson City, Nevada. Delivery promised within three weeks. Money-back guarantee. Plus a bonus poster of Alexandria in a bathing suit when the remittance was accompanied by ten new call signs.

"Steve Bringhurst?" she sputtered. "Call signs?"

She lifted her head in complete disbelief and, ignoring Zackery Quinn's maddening smile, proceeded to tear up every brochure on the desk and toss them in the wastebasket.

She turned on him then, her eyes ablaze with fury. "What else do you know about this that you haven't told me?"

He straightened to his full intimidating height. "I was hoping *you'd* tell me. They say confession is good for the soul."

Alex held her ground. "I confess nothing, except being related to a troubled teenager who...who I thought loved me." Her voice wobbled precariously. "Apparently I was wrong."

"Is that how you define love, Ms. Duncan? Forcing him to do your dirty work for you?" This time there was no mistaking the revulsion in his eyes.

CHAPTER SEVEN

"NOW WAIT A MINUTE!" Alex retorted, her hands on her hips. "There's definitely some dirty work going on here. But if you think for one second that I had any part in *that*—" her eyes darted to the wastebasket "—you're way off target. You'd better check your facts before you take the law into your own hands. As it is, I could sue you for defamation of character!"

His face looked as hard and impervious as rock. "Maybe I haven't made myself clear," he muttered with icy contempt. "*You're* the one who'll be going to court—for manipulating not one, but *three* minors in illegal mail-order activities. For operating without a business license. For not reporting your undisclosed earnings to the IRS—which will cost you a heavy fine, plus back taxes. For misusing the air waves of the ARRL to conduct illegal interstate, national and international business, which is an offense punishable by jail. For misuse of your guardianship rights. For contributing to the delinquency of a minor. Shall I go on?"

He'd lost her when he'd said that bit about the illegal mail-order activities. The rest she hadn't even taken in. At least, not yet. Fighting for control, she said in a strangely calm voice, "It looks like Troy and someone named Steve are involved. Who's the third minor, or am I supposed to guess?'' Her own anger made her immune to his black scowl.

''My nephew. Who else?''

''That's impossible! Troy didn't meet your nephew until he came out to your ranch this morning.''

''Wrong again.'' His eyes held an unholy gleam.

''He wouldn't lie to—'' Alex stopped herself mid-sentence, feeling the quicksand sucking her down. ''You have me at a disadvantage. I'm willing to concede that after seeing the evidence,'' she said in a shaky voice, ''and knowing that Troy lied to me about his whereabouts on the day I was out here taking photographs—'' she took a deep breath ''—anything is possible where my brother is concerned.''

''You sound so convincing you could probably pass a lie-detector test.''

Alex's chin came up. Staring him straight in the eye, she said, ''You're besotted by your own sense of self-importance, Mr. Quinn. You're setting yourself up as judge, jury and executioner. But you'd better be careful, because you don't have your facts straight.''

''Don't I?'' His eyes glittered. ''Do you deny that you arranged with Troy's shop teacher to set up a ham-radio set in your home and that you arranged for him to get his license?''

Was nothing sacred to Troy? Alex questioned inwardly. One day spent in this man's company and Troy had divulged their entire life history. ''No, I don't deny that my best friend's husband wanted to help Troy out of his depression after his football injury and offered to teach him.''

"Do you deny that you told Troy you were holding out until you could snag a rancher who would provide you with horses?"

She knew he could see the blush reddening her face and had already formed his own conclusion.

"I said that at a surprise birthday party my parents gave me when I was fourteen. I thought they'd bought me a horse, something I'd wanted for years. But instead, the gift turned out to be a book on the history of Arabians, because they couldn't afford to give me the real thing. And though I loved the book, it couldn't make up for my disappointment. My brother has teased me about it ever since."

There was a long silence while he apparently considered her explanation. "Do you deny you recognized me when I came into the Write Set-Up?"

"Look," she cried, "this is ridiculous! You know very well I admitted to seeing you at the horse show the year before."

"Do you deny that you knew my brother-in-law was the governor of our fair state?"

"*Yes!* At least until Troy told me over the phone."

His satisfied smile intensified. "Do you deny that you didn't know Randy was also involved in ham radio?"

"I'd never heard of Randy Cordell until just now! How on earth would I know if he had a ham radio or not?"

"Don't lie to me," he thundered. "A year ago Randy's name was in all the papers, including those in California, for possession of drugs."

Alex ran a hand through her hair in frustration. "Well, yes, now that you mention it, I do remember that, like any other citizen. But you're insinuating something else. Something entirely different."

"I'm doing more than that, Ms. Duncan. I'm accusing you of manipulating your brother to make contacts through ham radio in order to set up your illegal mail-order business. But unfortunately for you, when you made Randy one of your victims, you got in over your head."

Alex had never been so furious in her life. "I don't know what you're talking about! Why do you persist in believing the very worst about me?"

"Maybe it's because out of all the friends your brother made over the radio, he picked Steve—whose mother works evening shifts so she wouldn't know about her basement being used as a post office. And he picked Randy to fund his brochure. We know who encouraged him in both decisions. You chose Steve because you had to keep news of the mailings quiet, and Randy because you knew the wealth behind the Cordell family. You'd seen me at the horse show and you knew about my connection with the Cordells, so you figured you'd go for broke and snare yourself a rich rancher at the same time."

He ignored her outraged intake of breath. "The film, the mailing costs, and the kind of paper those posters are printed don't come cheap. But of course you had no more worries because wet-behind-the-ears Randy hocked everything valuable in his bedroom to keep the operation supplied with cash while *you*, Ms. Duncan, supplied the bait."

His voice grated. "And what beautiful bait it is."
He submitted her to a brazen appraisal reminiscent of
the one he'd given when he'd first entered the shop.
"There isn't a man alive who could remain indiffer-
ent to one of your posters. Certainly not the young
males throughout the U.S, Canada, Sweden and Germany, who now fantasize over your face and body
adorning their walls."

She was overwhelmed by what he was saying. She
couldn't have talked even if she'd known what to say.

Zackery Quinn continued relentlessly. "It seems
that before long, with the unwitting aid of that auto-
parts guy, Ron Sealey, you'll also have the Japanese
paying homage, to the tune of thousands of dollars.
Tell me—how much of a cut do you give your brother?
He does the work and all you have to do is stand
around looking sexy as hell."

Obeying blind instinct, Alex lunged for him and
slapped his face, hard. He grabbed her wrists in retal-
iation and dragged her against him.

Wrapping his hand in her flowing hair, he forced her
back, lowering his head so she could see the imprint of
her hand against the bronzed skin of his cheek. She
could feel his breath on her lips, and it sent a tremor
through her body.

"The truth hurts, doesn't it?" he snarled. "You've
been found out and your scam is at an end. Too bad
you didn't come to me directly. You could have had a
millionaire rancher without exploiting three young
vulnerable boys—one of whom holds the delicate position of being the governor's son. He also happens to
be the nephew I love. I protect my family, Ms. Dun-

can, and that includes Randy and Andrew Cordell. But make no mistake, I'd have paid your price for as long as you were offering."

In the next instant his mouth descended on hers and he began an assault on her senses that left her gasping and writhing in his arms. He knew exactly where and how to caress her. Terrified she might surrender to him, she shoved against his chest with both hands. But it was like trying to move a wall of granite.

"You're wrong about everything," she cried when his mouth released hers to kiss the hollow of her throat. "Don't you see? This has to be something Troy and Randy concocted themselves, with this boy Steve. Drive me out to the camp where they're sleeping and I'll prove it to you."

At first she was afraid she hadn't gotten through to him. His lips explored the side of her neck with drugging insistence before they swept over her hot cheek and claimed her mouth once more. He pulled away to demand, "You'd face both of them? Tonight?" His breath fanned lips made tender and swollen by the urgent pressure of his.

Just then he shifted her in his arms and she was able to break free of his hold, jerking with all her might. She put the back of her hand to her lips to stop the throbbing. When her eyes lifted to meet his gaze, she trembled at the violent passion she saw there.

"I want explanations much more than you do." Her voice shook from a welter of emotions. "It's *my* face on those posters, and if those boys have really been sending photographs of me in the mail—"

"Stop the playacting," he said, cutting off whatever she would have said. Like a magician he produced a large box from beneath his desk. "Are you trying to tell me you know nothing about *these?* That you didn't sign them?"

Swallowing hard, she counted at least three-dozen mailer tubes. Almost suffocating from the rage swelling inside her, she glanced at the addresses and estimated they represented twenty or more states. She pulled one tube out of the box, opened it and shook out the poster.

It showed her in bed reading, her hair piled high on her head after her shower, the ruffle on her nightgown perilously close to slipping off one shoulder. "To Chuck, Love, Alexandria," was written across the bottom.

Troy's handwriting.

"Please..." Her eyes beseeched him. "I have to talk to my brother tonight."

A sardonic smile lifted one corner of his mouth. He glanced at his watch. "It's late. After eleven."

"Then let me borrow one of your trucks. If you'll give me directions, I can find the boys myself."

His lip curled unpleasantly. "My own stockmen would have trouble this time of night, and Jocco could be any number of places." He seemed to take great delight in thwarting her.

"Are you saying you're not equal to the task?" She mimicked the question he'd asked her back at the shop. "Surely the king of the ranch can find a bunch of his stockmen bedded down for the night.

"Could it be that you're not quite so certain about my part in all this any more? Or," she added on a dangerous impulse, "is it that you've gotten rid of Troy and Randy, and they aren't even on the Circle Q? Anything's possible coming from you."

His eyes seemed mere pinpoints of light. "They're out there, Ms. Duncan, and we'll find them. Just don't forget you were the one who insisted."

"I haven't forgotten anything," was her frigid rejoinder.

"Touché." His sensuous tone implied that he was referring to something else, something more intimate. "Let's go." He gripped her elbow and steered her toward the doors.

But she suddenly remembered his father and pulled back. He eyed her suspiciously. "Why the hesitation?"

Shaking her head she said, "I-I've been hasty and selfish. And you're right, it is late. This can wait until morning when the boys return and we're all fresh."

In a lightning move he reached out and grasped her face in his hands, lifting it to his gaze. Not for the first time, she thought she saw a shadow of torment in his eyes, but it vanished too quickly for her to be certain. "I wondered how long it would take before you backed down. For a second there, I was actually beginning to believe you might be telling the truth."

"Y-you don't understand. If your father had a relapse and needed you and we didn't get back in time, I'd never forgive myself."

Another taut silence ensued. "How do you do that?" he asked in mock wonderment. "You sound so sincere.'' Dropping his hands from her face, he grabbed her wrist and started down the hallway with her in tow. She almost had to run to keep up with him. ''My father will live to see another day,'' he said in a hard voice. He led her out the main entry to the Range Rover and ushered her into it.

Emotionally drained and worn out from their verbal sparring, Alex lay back against the headrest and stared out her window. No words passed between them as he drove, negotiating the Rover along a rough track at high speed. They covered mile after mile of vast open range. From time to time, Alex caught sight of cattle in large peaceful herds.

The ranch by night had an element of magic. Despite the pain of Troy's disloyalty, despite the many unanswered questions—and worst of all, Zackery Quinn's bitter conviction that she had masterminded the boys' absurd mail-order business—despite all that, Alex couldn't help but be affected by the stark beauty of the landscape. The silhouette of the Sierra Nevadas loomed large in the background, and she could smell the heady scent of sage through the Rover's open windows.

The moon moved across the sky and still they drove. Alex's eyelids grew heavy and she fought to stay awake. Suddenly he slowed down, and she noticed cattle grazing on both sides of the track. She sat straighter in the seat, turning to look at him. ''Is something wrong?''

''We've passed several places where Jocco might have camped for the night. There's one spot I haven't checked, but it's another half hour away. I don't know about you, but I'm exhausted. We're going to camp here for the rest of the night. I always keep sleeping bags in the Rover, so we can use them. We'll start out at first light and catch up with them in time for breakfast."

Without asking her approval, he leapt down from the seat and began pulling things out of the back. "While I'm setting up the sleeping bags, you can get yourself ready for bed. Don't let the cattle frighten you. At this time of night they can't see your red hair and they're far more interested in eating their quota than chasing you."

His comment made her smile even though she was filled with conflicting emotions. "I may not have been born on a ranch, but I know about cows and they're color-blind."

He laughed out loud, a genuine laugh. It surprised her—and delighted her—so much her heart started to hammer painfully in her chest.

She watched from the Rover as Zack spread the sleeping bags side by side near an old camp-fire pit. The heat was still rising from the desert floor, but it would grow cool before morning, which was probably the reason he'd placed them so close together.

Ignoring the little shiver that raced up her spine, she got out of the car and walked over to one of the bags just as he wandered out of sight. She dropped to her knees, and removed her white high-heeled sandals and then she climbed into the sleeping bag. Her dress would be a wrinkled mess by morning.

"Do you want a drink before we go to sleep?"

His low voice startled her and she sat up, brushing the hair out of her eyes. "Yes, please."

He handed her a canteen and she swallowed thirstily, thinking water had never tasted so good.

After thanking him, she lay flat on her back staring up at glorious starry night. "Mr. Quinn?" she said tentatively when they were both settled for the night.

"What is it?" His back was to her, so his voice was muffled.

"I'm afraid of snakes."

After a long pause he said, "If that's an invitation for me to join you in your sleeping bag, I'd be more than happy to oblige. Unfortunately I'm afraid I'm too tired to perform to your expectations. For tonight, that is. Give me a few hours and I'm all yours, Ms. Duncan."

The man deserved to be drawn and quartered.

Alex turned on her stomach and buried her hot face in her arms. If the fates were kind, she'd be able to fall asleep quickly, without brooding about what her brother had done—or about what Zack Quinn had said.

It seemed she was granted her wish because when consciousness returned, she felt the cool air of morning on her face. Eyes still closed she enjoyed the feeling of well-being and warmth that enveloped her before she had to get up and meet the day. That was when she became aware of a silken caress running from the base of her spine to the nape of her neck, charging her body like a current of electricity.

Her eyes flew open and she discovered the upper half of her body lying against Zackery Quinn's chest, her face buried in his neck. Sometime during the night either he'd reached for her or her subconscious desires had driven her into his arms.

Embarrassed beyond words, she tried to move away from him, but his powerful arms were wrapped around her body. In the early light of dawn, she couldn't make out any details—except for his eyes, which smoldered between their dark lashes and set her heart tripping over itself.

His sensual smile took her breath away. "I could have used another hour's sleep, but I'm not complaining. I don't think you'll find anything to complain about, either," he said in a husky tone. As he spoke, his hands played with her hair, lifting the silken strands for the desert breeze to catch.

His gaze drifted over her features. Then his fingers traced the delicate arch of her brow. "Your eyes glow like the hearts of opals," he whispered. Suddenly his voice hardened. "You should wear a sign around that lovely neck. Warning—one look into these eyes could prove fatal."

Another arrow hit its mark, and she turned her face away from his relentless regard. "Whatever you believe, I didn't wake you intentionally."

"Of course you didn't." His low chuckle mocked her. "Just like you didn't plan to buy more time by keeping me fully occupied until both of us forgot why we were out on the range."

The cruelty of his sarcasm was too much. "Let me go!" She fought him in earnest, hot tears stinging her eyes. But in any kind of battle with him, she could never hope to win.

He flipped her onto her back so fast the world spun. "Maybe now you're learning the difference between pandering to teens and playing with men. It's a lesson you've been needing for a long time."

His mouth came down hard and crushed hers without tenderness. When he finally released her, his breath was ragged and hers nonexistent. "Before you lose your temper again, remember who was lying on top of whom when we woke up this morning." He let her go, then climbed out of his sleeping bag and rose to his feet. Running a hand through his black hair, he stared down at her with unreadable eyes.

Alex pushed the sleeping bag away and stood up, too, feeling slightly unsteady on her nylon-clad feet. She couldn't have cared less what she looked like, and she had to suppress a sudden hysterical urge to laugh as she noticed the audience of Herefords eyeing them balefully. "I can't wait till Troy and I are back in Reno," she said bitterly, "where we never have to see you or talk to you again."

"Troy might have something to say about that."

An icy coldness washed over Alex. She refused to dignify his remark with an answer. Instead, she searched for her shoes. As she started to slip them on, she caught sight of a truck on the horizon leaving a trail of dust in its wake.

"That'll be Jocco," he murmured, and in the time it took the truck to reach them, Alex had rolled up her sleeping bag and placed it in the back of the Range Rover. She needed some activity to channel the angry surge of adrenaline.

Her host handed her the canteen and walked over to the driver's side of the blue truck, which had pulled off the side of the track in front of them.

While his head was bent in conversation with his foreman, Alex watched a tall, lanky, brown-haired young man, who bore a faint resemblance to his uncle, alight from the back of the truck. With slightly more difficulty, Troy followed using his crutches, his sandy hair with its tinge of red blowing in the breeze. The two of them were bantering with each other like old buddies. As Troy greeted Zackery Quinn his face broke into a broad smile, and he shook his hand with a look of adoration on his face. Troy had had the time of his life, all right, she thought.

From where she stood at the rear of the Range Rover, Alex stared hard at her brother. The impact of what he'd done struck her anew. She wondered if she'd ever really known him.

As Jocco started up the truck and began to drive off down the track, leaving his two young passengers behind, Alex stepped out from her sheltered position near the Rover and walked toward them.

Troy's face froze when he turned his head to say something to his friend and saw her. *"Alex!"* He darted a furtive glance at Zack, then at the nephew, before staring at her once more. "W-what are you doing out here? How did you get here so fast?"

"I drove straight to the ranch as soon as I got your message."

He shook his head. His face wore his defensive mind-your-own-business look. "Why? I said I'd be home in a few days. What's the big deal?"

She took a deep breath. "That's very interesting, considering you told Bruce and all your friends back in Grass Valley that you couldn't go with them for their camp-out—because the doctor hadn't given his permission for you to leave the house yet."

His tongue distended his cheek, another telltale sign that he didn't like the way this conversation was going. "That's because I didn't want to go with them but I didn't want to hurt their feelings. Look, Alex, do you think we could talk about this some other time?" By now, his blue eyes were sending her a silent plea.

"When I told Mr. Quinn why I needed to talk to you," she said, "he was kind enough to drive me out here. Since this . . . problem concerns the four of us, I don't see why we shouldn't discuss it now. Mr. Quinn is a very busy man and his time is valuable."

"The four of us?" Troy's face screwed up in a frown.

"Five, actually, but Steve Bringhurst isn't around. Funny, I'd never heard of him before last night, never met him, but apparently he's a trusted friend of yours. I'd like to make his acquaintance one day."

Ignoring her brother's shocked expression, she let her gaze travel to a sheepish-looking Randy. She stepped forward. "No one has introduced us yet, Randy, or should I call you Jerry? Jerry Spaulding, isn't it? That's what it said on the box." At that point Troy's head jerked around and he stared at his friend as though Randy had just sprouted an extra head. "Randy, have you told Troy you go by an alias?"

Throughout the long silence she felt rather than saw Zackery Quinn draw closer.

"No," the other boy finally admitted, and Troy looked dazed.

"Well, I'm not surprised. With your father being the governor, I doubt he'd be too thrilled to know his son and my brother and someone else's son have been using ham radio to drum up money on the side. But I'm getting ahead of myself."

She smiled coldly. "In case you didn't recognize me, Randy, from all those posters you boys have been sending all over the world, I'm Alexandria. I apologize for the way I look this morning. It's been a rough night all round."

Zackery Quinn didn't move or even change his stance, but his facial muscles tautened. Pretending not to notice, she extended her hand to Randy who had the grace to blush before he shook it.

She stepped back and looked her brother directly in the eye. "From what I understand, you guys have a fantastic business going. Twenty-five dollars a poster isn't bad, but since I was an economics major at the university, you should have consulted me—I would have told you to jack it up to forty dollars. If people have to pay more money for something, they tend to consider it more valuable, you know. Oh, yes, Troy, Dad would have been really proud of the way you've put the Write Set-Up on the map. And what's so nice about it is that you've kept it in the family."

By now both boys had gone pale, and Troy looked positively ill. "You know, little brother, if I'd realized that the pictures you kept taking around the house—supposedly for practice—would sell so well, I could have put on nice clothes and makeup and posed for them.''

Troy kept swallowing. "I'm sorry, Alex." His voice came out in a whisper.

"I'm sorry, too. And you want to know something funny? When Mr. Quinn came to our shop asking us to do an ad for Domino, he really came to investigate *me.*"

She noticed the strange glitter in Zack's eyes as she gestured toward him. "You see, he believes I not only posed for those pictures, but that I put you up to it."

At that remark, Troy shot Randy a horrified glance.

"He also believes I abused my rights as your guardian by forcing you to find someone who had a lot of money, like Randy, to back you in my under-cover venture."

"That's crazy!" Troy cried, staring at the rancher as if he wasn't quite so perfect, after all. It warmed her heart to see that some loyalty remained.

"In fact, he thinks I've been planning this scheme since I attended the horse show in Reno last year. I saw him there, and he believes I made the connection with his brother-in-law."

"Jeez," both boys moaned, and Troy closed his eyes.

"I'm sorry," he muttered again and Randy looked as if he wanted to crawl into a hole. "All I wanted to do was earn enough money on my own so you wouldn't have to work so hard and put your life on hold for me."

Alex bit her lower lip, which was still tender from Zackery Quinn's last kiss, but the tears came, anyway. "I believe you." Her voice trembled. "The only problem is, Mr. Quinn doesn't believe *me*. So that's why I'm going to get in his car and wait while the three of you take it from here. Is that all right with you, Mr. Quinn?" she asked, noticing he didn't look quite so hostile anymore.

Heaving a deep shuddering sigh, she smoothed a stray strand of hair away from her face. "I'm through trying to defend myself, boys, so please come clean to Mr. Quinn about everything before you join me. I don't want him to have any excuse ever to come near me or my office again. As for you, Troy, I'd say it's vitally important to be honest with him if you want to remain on his payroll."

"Alex . . ." Her brother tried to speak but she was beyond listening.

"It's all right, Troy. You've needed someone to confide in. Why not Mr. Quinn? He's a man of strong moral convictions. In fact, he's been teaching me the error of my ways. So you'll be in good hands. I can see now that I haven't given you the freedom to grow up. I apologize for that. What can a sister teach a brother about being a man?"

"Alex . . ." he pleaded with tears in his voice.

"I have a business to run in Reno, and I need to get back there as soon as possible, so don't take too long sorting things out. Okay?"

As she started to walk away, Troy called her name once more. She heard the need and the pain, but she couldn't respond because her own need, her own pain, was killing her.

CHAPTER EIGHT

"YOU SAID YOUR SISTER would kill us if she ever found out." Randy spoke first. "You weren't kidding. I feel like the biggest jerk that ever lived."

Troy hunched over his crutches. "She'll never forgive me and I don't blame her. She doesn't think I love her and she couldn't be more wrong. Too bad I wasn't killed out on that football field. Then none of this would have happened. What a mess." His voice broke.

"Mess" didn't adequately describe the situation. Zack felt—Lord, he couldn't begin to describe how he felt. His sickness of heart, his self-loathing. He'd been out of control from the moment he'd seen her photographs, and he realized now that the blackness he'd had in his soul for so many years was responsible for the escalation of what should have been a minor crisis, easily put to rights.

"It's going to be okay, boys." He put a comforting arm around each of them, desperate for a large dose of comfort himself. "Her anger was directed at me, not you. Right now she needs a little time."

"A little..." Randy stared up at his uncle in disbelief. "She's so furious it's scary."

"That's because she's got red hair," the rancher said calmly.

"For crying out loud, Uncle Zack."

"You know, Randy, he's right." Zack heard the hope that sprang into Troy's voice. "I'd forgotten." He sniffed. "Mom had red hair, and Dad always used to say she needed more time than other people to cool off."

"What else did your dad say?" Zack tousled Troy's hair and smiled at him, praying for a little wisdom right about now.

"They didn't fight very often. But when they did, it was a doozie. Dad would just leave her alone and not even try to talk to her. Instead, he'd do lots of nice things for her and make us help. Pretty soon, she'd get over the worst of it and start talking to him again. When that happened, he'd always tell us to go stay at friends' houses for the weekend. Stuff like that." His voice trailed off in embarrassment.

A lump lodged in Zack's throat. Mixed in with his own sense of guilt and shame was a growing attachment to the boy whose home had been filled with so much love before tragedy struck.

"I think I'll take a leaf out of your dad's book, Troy. Let's all get in the Rover and head back to the house. Your sister had car trouble after she got here and my mechanic should have it fixed by now. If she's got clients this morning in Reno, then she's going to have to hurry, and I don't want to hold her up any longer."

"Zack?" Troy had to shield his eyes to look at him, because a blinding sun had come up over the Sierras. "I'm going back to Reno with Alex."

Zack nodded. "I'm glad you said that, because I was going to suggest it if you didn't. She needs you right now."

"Will you hold that job open for me in case she ever talks to me again and gives her permission?"

"Do you even have to ask? We're friends, aren't we?"

"Yeah." The first semblance of a smile appeared.

"Do you really think we'll ever see the day when she forgives any of us?" Randy interjected pessimistically.

That was the question Zack had been asking himself over and over, like a litany. He didn't appreciate his nephew's reminding him of the long ordeal ahead. He had to start over with Alex, but there could be no guarantees, not after the unforgivable things he'd said and done to her.

"You haven't seen the real Alex, Randy. Normally my sister is the sweetest person on earth."

Zack had seen that sweetness manifested in a dozen different ways since he'd first met her. He'd been profoundly touched by her concern over his father, though he had refused to acknowledge it at the time. Then there was the way she'd handled the horses, winning them over with kindness and a gentle voice. And the wondering awe in her startlingly beautiful eyes when he'd shown her the eagle.

"I've been the world's biggest jerk," Troy said, echoing Randy's self-deprecating words.

"Well, it's over now, boys. I have faith that you two and this Steve can close down your operation. You need to pay all outstanding debts and return any money you've received. Nothing more needs to be said about it. Shall we go?''

As they walked to the Rover, Zack saw the woman whose image had robbed him of sleep since the first time he'd seen that poster. She sat in the front passenger seat staring out the window. He climbed in beside her and the boys got into the back. He couldn't help noticing her awful stillness, and it chilled him.

He turned the key in the ignition and while the engine idled, he reached for the car phone. After calling Yolanda and learning his father had spent a restful night, he called his mechanic to make certain Ms. Duncan's car was in front of the ranch house ready for travel.

Zack would have flown her back to Reno himself, but he knew that in her present state of mind she'd accept nothing from him, not even breakfast, although she must have been famished.

As for him, he felt as if he'd just contracted a fatal illness and would never eat, drink, laugh or find joy in anything again.

Not until she came willingly into his arms.

Helpless to do otherwise, he turned his head and saw her profile. Her very remoteness filled him with a fear he'd never known before. The kind he could taste, the kind that permeated every cell of his body. *The fear of loss . . .*

''ALEX? I JUST WANTED you to know I'm leaving for my job now.''

She was surprised at the announcement, since they'd only been back from the ranch one day and a night. During that time they'd been civil to each other and nothing more. She stopped what she was doing—laying out an ad—long enough to look up at her brother.

His eyes betrayed his anxiety, and she could imagine what was coming next. Zackery Quinn was probably outside the shop waiting to take Troy to his ranch for the summer. Alex had made no demur when her brother got into the car with her for the ride back home, though she had to admit she was surprised. She had thought he'd stay behind. She knew there was nothing he wanted more than to work for Zackery Quinn and live on his ranch. In fact, there'd been a time when she'd fantasized almost the same thing for herself. *To be loved by him and to live out the rest of her days with him...*

"You're going to leave without a suitcase?" she asked.

He stood there leaning on his crutches, his face screwed up in pain that was reminiscent of the day before. "No. Not the circle Q. I called Ron Sealey early this morning and he told me he'd be by for me at nine-thirty." Troy glanced at his watch. "It's almost that now."

"No, Troy. I won't let you do it." Concern for him and his needless self-sacrifice brought her to her feet. "He's the last person I want you to work for. You were right about him. He's hoping to get close to me through you. And you'd die of boredom in the back room of his store, looking up model numbers on parts."

"I'm not in the mail-order business anymore and I need a job."

"You've been offered one. A good one. All you have to do is pick up the phone and tell Mr. Quinn you accept." She didn't imagine the burst of joy that flared in his blue eyes at the mere mention of the cattle king's name. "I'll drive you to the airport—I'm sure he'll be glad to arrange a flight to his ranch. Or maybe he'll want to come for you himself and bring Randy. But first you need to call Mr. Quinn and then pack your clothes. I'll take care of Ron Sealey—maybe invite him over for dinner tonight so I can explain. I think he'll understand..."

Troy looked shaken. "Are you serious?"

"Perfectly."

It was when she smiled that he dropped his crutches and hobbled toward her. She winced to see him walking on his bad leg and rushed forward to stop him. He embraced her tightly, smelling faintly of the cologne their father had always worn.

That started her tears, and seeing them, Troy confessed in a halting voice that Steve had driven up from Carson City the day Alex was out. Troy had gone back to Steve's house with him to work on the mailings. After he'd asked—and received—her forgiveness for the dozenth time, they were both startled by the sound of a horn honking out front.

"Must be Ron," she said, wiping her eyes. "I'll go talk to him. And you get on the phone and call the Circle Q."

A few minutes' worth of explanation and an invitation for a seafood dinner seemed to pacify Ron, who told her that sounded great and he'd be by at seven. She hoped he wouldn't get the wrong idea. She'd have to make it clear that there couldn't be anything but friendship between them. He was a nice person, attractive, and it wouldn't hurt to have a meal together, but that was it.

She really did need more of a social life, especially since she'd be living alone for the summer. Maybe she'd start accepting dates with the men who came into the shop and asked her out. There were also the male friends Vicky and Sally were dying to introduce her to.

It all sounds awful, she thought. And the rest of her life she didn't even want to think about. She couldn't. Not when the image of one man blotted out the rest.

As she went back into the shop, Troy was just finishing his phone conversation, an expression of excitement on his face.

He said goodbye and put down the receiver. "Randy and Pete are coming for me in an hour!"

"Then you'd better get busy packing." It seemed that Zack didn't want to risk seeing her, after all. Alex had to fight the emotions that suddenly overwhelmed her. She'd take her lunch hour when the others were due to arrive and run to the grocery store for fresh fish and salad vegetables. That way she'd avoid running into anyone connected with the Circle Q.

It didn't take Troy long to get his gear packed, including his fishing rod and his Walkman. When she was ready to leave for the store, Troy walked out to the car with her.

"Zack told me I could phone you whenever I wanted for free."

She wondered if the mention of his name would always bring that sharp pain. "You don't have to call me all the time, Troy. Just give me a quick call once in a while so I know everything's okay, especially with your leg."

He leaned into the car and kissed her cheek. "Thanks. You're the best sister a guy ever had—and I'll spend the rest of my life making it up to you."

She flashed him a mock frown. "What are you trying to do? Put me on a permanent guilt trip?"

He sobered. "No. I just can't believe you're taking this so well after everything I did."

"Your heart was in the right place, Troy. Let's chalk it up to experience and go on from there."

"I take back every mean thing I ever said about you. You're going to make a great mom someday."

She put her key in the ignition and started the engine. "I'll have to be a great wife first, and that simply isn't going to happen. Have fun and don't break another leg."

He kissed her again and she drove off, determined to be nowhere near the shop when they came for Troy.

ANXIOUS TO TALK to his best friend, Zack took the steps two at a time and entered the foyer of the Biscay Inn. Miguel's mother waved when she saw him. "Zack! You've stayed away too long. Come over here so we can have a talk. Miguel's in the back, but he'll have to wait."

"Begona." He moved behind the counter and gave her a warm hug. Though they shared no blood ties, she was as close to him as an aunt, and he loved her despite her implacability on certain issues. "How are you? How are Perocheguy and Irena?"

"My husband's arthritis keeps him home more, but I'm not complaining, not when I think of your poor papa. My daughter is the same as always. She'll take over for me in the dining room on Tuesday so I can drop in on your papa and tell him all the latest ranching gossip."

"Bless you." Zack kissed her forehead. "And thank Irena for me. Dad has always enjoyed your company and he looks forward to every visit." He paused, then added quietly, "I don't think he'll last much longer."

Begona crossed herself, then patted his arm. "You don't look so good. What's going on with you, besides your papa?"

After a long silence he said, "You don't want to know."

"Ah, then it's woman trouble." She threw up her hands.

"Why is it that happiness has eluded my favorite boy? Can you answer me that? Why aren't you married and expecting a baby like Miguel and Marieli?"

Zack grimaced. "Because I'm a fool," he said abruptly. "I'll see you Tuesday, Begona." He brought an end to their conversation, having no desire to discuss Miguel's marriage when she understood so little about her own son or Marieli. Nor did he want to discuss Miguel's private agonies, which had their roots deep in complicated family issues originating in the Pyrenees at the turn of the century.

After giving her another hug, he walked through the main dining room, nodding to several people he knew on the way to the private room reserved for members of Miguel's huge extended family. His well-to-do Basque relatives tended to stick together, and they frequently used the Biscay to conduct their daily business.

Miguel was standing by the window with a bleak look on his face. When he saw Zack, he exclaimed, "Thank heaven it's you! Let's get out of here."

Zack nodded. "I'll fly us back to the ranch, and we'll go for a long ride. That way we can be assured of privacy. I have to talk to you, or I'll go insane. Can you take that much time off?"

"Whether I can or not, I'm going to," Miguel declared firmly. "There's been a new development, and I need your advice. But before we talk about me, I want to hear what's happened to you. Did you finally get a confession out of her brother?"

"You could say that. Yesterday, everything came to a head, and I learned that Alex has been the innocent victim in all this—just as she claimed. Randy and Troy and Steve cooked up the whole scheme without her knowledge. Now that the truth has come out, she's through with me." His voice was grim. "I've lost her, Miguel. What I did to her is unforgivable. The chances of her ever speaking to me again are practically nonexistent and... and I'm terrified."

Miguel raked a hand through his black hair and stared at Zack for a long unsmiling moment. "If you feel that strongly, then don't let her get away. Do whatever it takes." There was more emotion in his voice than Zack had ever heard before.

"I've already put a plan into action, but it probably doesn't have a hope in hell of succeeding."

"If I were you, I wouldn't let it stop there. Bombard her until she gets the message."

Zack could hear the pain in Miguel's words. "What new development were you referring to a moment ago?"

"I'll tell you after we get out to the ranch. Too many ears around here. Besides, I do my best thinking on the back of a horse."

THE DAY TURNED OUT to be a busy one for Alex, with a steady stream of customers and phone calls in the afternoon. She didn't have a spare minute to think about the impact of Troy's absence or Zackery Quinn's treatment of her.

She understood that, after seeing the photographs, he had every right to be upset over Randy and Troy's illegal activities, every right to be suspicious of her. But to carry out such an elaborate plan of revenge, instead of simply approaching her to ascertain the facts displayed a cruel streak she couldn't explain or forgive.

So why was she feeling this devastating loss? She didn't understand it. Maybe there was something perverse in her nature that despised Zackery Quinn's tactics yet needed his touch. She'd never forget the sense of completeness and belonging that had swept over her every time he'd taken her in his arms.

What disturbed her most of all was the knowledge that no other man would ever be able to claim her inner heart, because Zackery Quinn had gotten there first. He'd burned his brand so deeply there was no room for anyone else.

The thought terrified her, and she plunged into her work with frenetic energy in an attempt to blot the memory of him from her mind.

Around four o'clock an Express Air delivery man came in while she was helping a customer. He handed her a packet, asked her to sign for it and left. She didn't get an opportunity to see what was inside until she'd closed and locked the front door at six. Ron would be arriving within the hour, so she had to hurry.

A folded document slid from the envelope. "The Registry" stood out in bold type on the front, under the silhouette of an Arabian horse head. "What on earth?" She lifted the flap and discovered a note, with a key taped to it, inside:

Alex—
I knew you wouldn't take money for your photographic work at the ranch. Please accept Snow White as payment, instead—and consider her a very belated fourteenth birthday present. She's right outside your shop, waiting for you to love her.

She's a beautiful six-month-old filly sired by Domino. Her mother is Snowfire. Their ancestry is registered in the Polish Arabian Stud Book. Now that she's been weaned, her temporary home is Jack Werrett's Stud Farm in Sparks. Give him a call anytime and he'll take good care of both of you. If you decide you don't want her or can't accept her, then she's yours to sell or give away.
                                        —Zack Quinn

Alex thought she must be hallucinating. But when

she spread the document out flat on the counter, it read, "To Alexandria Fitzroy Duncan, OWNER. Purebred Arabian Horse. Certificate of Registration. Arabian Horse Registry of America, Inc."

Beneath was a list of the horse's markings and pedigree, with the owner's registered number, the sex of the foal, time of birth and name of witness.

Like a person moving under water, Alex picked up the note and reread it. According to this, the filly was *right outside!* But that was impossible! You didn't just deposit a horse on someone's doorstep. This had to be some kind of joke!

But what if it wasn't?

With her heart thumping like an off-balance washing machine, she left the document lying on the counter and hurried over to the door she'd just locked. Her fingers wouldn't function properly and she was out of breath when she finally flung it open.

The first thing she saw was a brand-new brown-and-white one-horse trailer, no vehicle attached to it, parked beside the curb under a chestnut tree.

It was there in front of her eyes and she *still* didn't believe it! But by now she should have learned that Zackery Quinn always meant what he said, and only a man of his means and resources had the power to do something so incredible, so extraordinary.

Who knew how long the trailer had been there? Sometime during the afternoon, an employee from the Circle Q had been out in front of the Write Set-Up, and she hadn't even known about it.

Galvanized into action by the realization that the horse might be frightened, Alex dashed back for the key, then flew across the front lawn and unlocked the rear door of the trailer.

"Oh!" she cried in absolute awe when her eyes adjusted to the interior light. There, in the straw shavings, stood a steel-gray Arabian with a darker mane and tail and three white stocking feet.

"You gorgeous thing," she murmured in soothing tones. The haltered filly, startled by her presence, trembled beneath her stroking hand. But she soon calmed down, whinnying gently when Alex reached into the hay net and urged the filly to eat.

Arabians were people-lovers, which was why Alex particularly liked them. She felt positively maternal as the horse accepted her ministrations with no sign of balking or skittishness. She'd obviously been well-trained.

Though the filly was gray now, when she grew older she'd be white like her parents. Like Domino. Alex couldn't think of the prized show horse without seeing Zackery Quinn's sun-bronzed face, his lean powerful body, his fluid effortless movements.

Alex was roused from the thoughts that had been plaguing her all day when the filly lifted her head and butted Alex's stomach, her affectionate nature already in evidence.

"Are you thirsty?" She chuckled and rubbed the horse's nose, trying to harden her heart against Zackery Quinn's bribery. Snow White had to be the most beautiful creature in the world. Alex could hardly stand to tear herself away long enough to get the horse some water.

"I'll be right back," she promised, then ran to the house for a bucket. While she was filling it from the garden hose, a Sealey Auto Parts truck pulled up ahead of the trailer.

Ron! She'd completely forgotten.

The next ten minutes were a kind of a blur as Alex gave the horse some water, all the while apologizing to Ron for not having dinner ready. Skipping over certain relevant details and avoiding the name of Snow White's donor, she explained that a client had just given her a horse in lieu of payment. Of course she couldn't accept, she told Ron. Then she excused herself to call Werrett's, where the horse would be boarded, to come and get her.

Ron told her she'd be crazy not to keep the filly, but he offered to hitch the trailer to his truck and pull it to the stables for her. They could do that on their way to dinner. He knew of a great Chinese restaurant in Sparks, he said, adding that she could give him a home-cooked meal next time.

Oh, no, she thought. She should never have started this with him, but he'd been so understanding about Troy's other job offer, she felt she owed him dinner at the very least. With his tennis-player build and blond good looks, not to mention his outgoing personality, Ron ought to be the kind of man she could date. But even before she'd met Zackery Quinn, the chemistry between her and Ron just wasn't there—not on her end, anyway—and she didn't want to be beholden to him for anything else.

However, Snow White's needs had to be met and Ron was here, insisting on helping out. In the end they drove to the stud farm, where Jack Werrett greeted Alex like visiting royalty.

"Zack told me to expect a call from you," the older man said. "My son, Arnie, was all set to come out to your house and haul the trailer for you." He greeted Ron with a cordial handshake, then gazed at Alex, giving her a warm friendly smile. "So you're the lucky lady." His eyes twinkled. "Did you know that Snow White is Domino's first offspring? There isn't a horse-lover around here who wouldn't give his eyeteeth to own her. Zack said all along she wasn't for sale, but I guess he had a right to change his mind. I think I can see why."

Alex could tell what thoughts were going through the man's head, and there was no way to disabuse him. Worse, she'd been vague about everything with Ron, who couldn't help picking up on Mr. Werrett's insinuations, making the situation that much more complicated.

"If you could tell me where to take Snow White, I'll put her to bed for the night."

"Third stall on the left in the barn directly behind you. Let me know if you need anything."

Alex thanked him, then opened the back of the trailer. While Ron held the door, Alex untied the rope and helped the filly back carefully out. Snow White seemed happy to be on firm ground. She kept nudging Alex's cotton shirt as if she wanted to play. Alex laughed and raised her arms to hold the horse's head steady for a minute. "You're as beautiful as your namesake. Look, Ron!" she called over her shoulder. "She has a strip!"

He moved next to her and grasped the rope so that his hand overlapped hers. "What's a strip?" he asked, a half smile on his lips. He was looking at Alex with a great deal more interest than he'd shown in the horse—exactly what she'd hoped to avoid.

"It's a white line running down the top of her nose. One day she'll be white all over." A deep familiar voice spoke from behind them.

Alex jumped and felt the blood pound in her ears. *Not him! Not now!* Where had he come from? He was supposed to be at the Circle Q with Troy and Randy.

She pulled her hand free of Ron's and turned around. Not because she wanted to, she told herself, but because she couldn't very well ignore the man who'd made total chaos of her life. The man who stood there demanding to be acknowledged.

Dressed in a Western-cut suit of a light brown twill with a darker shirt open at his throat, Zackery Quinn looked unbearably handsome, every inch the powerful owner of the Circle Q.

"Good evening, Alex." Her first name, said in that husky tone, made her breath catch. Although twilight had come upon them, she glimpsed a burning darkness in his eyes. His gaze dwelt possessively on her mouth as he said, "It seems like years ago, instead of yesterday morning, that we watched the sun come up over the Sierras together."

CHAPTER NINE

"AREN'T YOU GOING to introduce us, Alex?" he said before she could recover. He extended a hand toward the man at her side. "You must be Ron Sealey. Troy told me about the mix-up. Some time ago I offered him a job on my ranch and we only finalized things this morning. I hope there aren't any hard feelings."

"None at all," Ron said, shaking the rancher's hand. He was no longer smiling.

Alex clutched Snow White's rope with tense fingers, and the filly drew closer, as if she sensed a crisis building and wanted to comfort Alex.

"Ron..." She had to clear her throat before she could go on. "This is Zackery Quinn, owner of the Circle Q Ranch near Yerington."

"That's right." The friendly smile Zack flashed at Ron would have fooled anyone but Alex. She'd been shaken by the look he gave her before he switched his gaze to Ron. It had been frank with longing, stirring up feelings she'd tried to suppress. "When I approached the Write Set-Up to do an ad featuring Snow White's sire, Domino, I had no idea what Alex and Troy were capable of turning out."

His dark eyes slid to hers once more, reminding her, in the growing darkness, of banked fires that still smoldered. "It surpassed my expectations. I didn't think a check in the mail would convey my appreciation in quite the same way as this filly." There was a slight pause before he directed his gaze to the other man. "Are you a horse lover, Ron?"

"Can't say that I am," was the terse reply. Alex could feel the tension increasing by the minute.

"Ah, well, Alex shares my passion for horses." Zack went on talking as though he and Ron were old friends. "She even had my stallion, Pasha, eating out of her hand the other day when we went riding. A horse's instincts are never wrong, you know. Unlike some men—whose better instincts get clouded by other issues." His voice dropped several degrees and his solemn gaze captured Alex's. "I'd never give up Snow White to anyone in whom I didn't have complete trust."

Her heart started to pound heavily. If this was his way of apologizing, it still wouldn't work. Those other issues had turned him into a forbidding stranger, one *she* couldn't trust. There'd been something ugly, almost fanatical, about his accusations, something that had gone beyond mere hurt. He'd injured her so deeply she doubted the wounds would ever completely heal.

Lifting her head, she eyed him steadily. "I can't keep her, Mr. Quinn."

"The name is Zack. We got way beyond the formalities yesterday morning, wouldn't you say?" he reminded her with brutal honesty, obviously uncaring that Ron could hear every word. Alex sensed her companion's patience had reached its end.

As if to set a match to kindling, Zack reached for the rope, covering Alex's hand as the other man had done. Worse, he was running his index finger along the side of her wrist with urgent insistence, fanning the fire burning inside her. A benign smile broke out on his face. "Ron, I have a few matters to discuss with Alex about the filly. Why don't you go and park the trailer next to the barn while Alex and I are... otherwise occupied? I won't keep her long."

"That's good," Ron replied with an icy smile. "Alex and I have a dinner engagement." He stood his ground admirably well, Alex thought, groaning to herself, but Ron was no match for Zackery Quinn. No man was.

"I'll hurry, Ron," she hastened to assure him, not wanting this charade to continue a second longer than necessary.

Jerking her hand free, she struck out for the barn at a brisk pace and could hear the sound of the filly's hooves close behind.

When she reached the empty stall, Alex spun around, her cheeks on fire. "I told you I can't keep her," she blurted out, all pretense of civility gone.

He didn't respond, but calmly removed the halter from Snow White's neck and ran a practiced hand over her back, settling her in for the night.

Alex's eyes closed tightly as she remembered that same caress running along *her* back yesterday morning, filling her with a desire she'd never known before.

"If your schedule at the Write Set-Up keeps you too busy to drive here on a regular basis, I'll have her moved to the ranch where Troy can take care of her for you. He's as crazy about horses as you are."

"I'd prefer you didn't do that. He'd grow too attached to her and you'd only succeed in making my brother long for things he can't have."

"I've already struck a bargain with him," he told her in an even voice. "Part of his wages will be held back to invest in a horse. By summer's end, he'll have a two-year-old of his own. He'll be able to ride after his cast comes off. Taking care of Snow White could teach him what he needs to learn and solve a problem for you at the same time." This was said while he was down on his haunches inspecting Snow White's left hind leg.

"I can't do anything about Troy, but I refuse to be beholden to you, Mr. Quinn. For anything!"

"You own the horse, Alex," he stated, getting to his feet, his eyes trapping hers. Some power seemed to prevent her from looking away. "I guess your only alternative is to sell her. Since you don't want her at the ranch, you don't have much choice but to keep her boarded here until you can find a new owner. The fee is paid up through August."

"You've thought of everything, haven't you?" she lashed out. "Nothing is beyond the great Zackery Quinn's mighty reach. No mountain too high to scale."

His slow smile sent her pulse racing. Unable to withstand his knowing glance, she averted her eyes.

"I'm glad you understand me so well. As you might expect, Snow White will bring top dollar. Enough to invest for a secure future. Jack will advise you on a reasonable asking price and check out any potential buyers. I know I can count on you to choose someone who'll have Snow White's best interests at heart,'' he said smoothly.

Alex was still too furious—and too confused—to speak. "She's had all her shots," he went on, "and she's and has been dewormed. If you haven't sold her within six weeks, she'll need to go through the same process again. Bryan Watkins is the vet here and he'll see to everything." He patted Snow White's hind quarters. "I believe that covers what I needed to discuss with you. Please convey my apologies to Ron for spoiling your dinner date." He paused, eyebrows raised. "It's a shame he doesn't know what I overheard Troy tell Randy on the radio."

Alex ignored him and turned to leave. But a hand gripped her arm, holding her in place. He smiled wolfishly.

"Don't you think Ron should know he was never even in the running?" he said. "Why don't you put the poor guy out of his misery and tell him you're already spoken for?"

Alex would have refuted his declaration, but he dragged her hard against him and stifled her mouth with his own. She could feel the taut sinew of his thighs, the solid strength of his chest.

"Lord, I've been waiting for this," he muttered feverishly as he covered her face and mouth with kisses. What began as a battle of wills erupted into an explosion of aching need. Alex couldn't remember when she stopped fighting him and gave in to her own cravings. It seemed all he had to do was touch her and she forgot everything except this rush of feeling only he could satisfy.

"Alex?" The minute she heard Ron call her name, she broke away from Zack's grasp. "What's holding you up?" Ron sounded upset. She couldn't blame him.

Alex backed against the wall, fighting to get her breathing under control. Zack put his hands on either side of her face, preventing movement. She couldn't have answered Ron just then if her life depended on it.

"Will you tell him, or shall I?" Zack whispered before capturing her mouth once more in a kiss that left her breathless. "You know where you want to spend the rest of the night," he murmured against her lips, "and it isn't with him."

Zack's arrogance in assuming she was his for the asking made her aware of her surroundings. How could she let him do this to her when she knew his dark side, knew how dangerous he could be? How could she continue to kiss him like this when Ron was her date for the evening? Ron, who was growing more irritated and suspicious with every second that passed.

"I'm coming!" She found her voice at last and escaped Zack's hold, breaking into a run as she headed for the door of the barn.

"Have fun, you two." Zack's laconic remark coming on the heels of her flight from his arms infuriated Alex. And it seemed to infuriate Ron just as much. He didn't say anything, but his motions spoke for him as he accompanied her to his truck. His pace was brisk and angry. She could tell from the set of his features that he wished Zackery Quinn on the far side of the moon.

After a few minutes driving, Alex realized Ron had headed back to Reno. "Aren't we going to have dinner first?"

"I'd like to, if I thought you wanted to be with me," he said in a quiet voice. "Why did you bother to invite me to dinner in the first place? It's pretty obvious you and the big rancher have something going."

Alex felt terrible. "I know that's how it must look, but it's not what you think."

"Give me a break," he muttered. "That filly must be worth a hundred thousand dollars. No man parts with money like that unless he has a vested interest— not even a man with as much money as Zackery Quinn. Besides, I saw the way he looked at you." A harsh laugh broke from him. "He was like Attila the Hun dividing up the spoils, taking you for his prize and letting the hordes know it in case anyone dared to have other ideas."

Alex couldn't dispute anything Ron said, because deep down she knew he spoke the truth.

Ron sighed. "I'd give him a run for his money if I thought there was a chance you didn't return his feelings. But you do, don't you?"

She liked Ron too much to lie to him. "I . . . I admit there's an attraction, but it's one I'd give anything not to feel."

"Thanks for that much honesty," he said without rancor. "It's more than my ex-wife ever gave me."

When they reached her house, Alex turned to him. "Thank you for helping me with Snow White. I really mean this when I say I wished things had worked out differently."

"So do I. Good luck, Alex."

OVER THE NEXT TWO WEEKS, Alex spent every bit of her spare time with Snow White. She was so busy she hardly had a chance to miss Troy. With him gone, she felt no guilt about leaving the house right after work and not returning until ten or later.

She had every intention of selling the horse and always told herself that *this* time she'd speak to Jack Werrett about making the arrangements. But she hadn't counted on her growing attachment to Snow White. The filly seemed to adore Alex and had learned to rely on her nightly visits. From the beginning, she'd follow Alex everywhere without a lead rope. And she rebelled like any child when it was time to go to bed.

Every night when she returned Snow White to her stall, Alex found it harder and harder to consider parting with the horse. She worried that another owner might not treat her right or give her the time and attention she deserved.

By the third week, Alex couldn't lie to herself any longer. There was no way she could give up the animal. Except for Troy's weekly call, Alex heard nothing from the Circle Q and decided that whatever had gone on between her and the rancher was over. On his part, at least.

After the way he'd treated her, she should have been relieved to be left alone. But one Saturday night, for no apparent reason, Alex flung her arm around the filly's neck and sobbed quietly. Snow White whinnied as if she understood.

"Alex?"

She lifted her tearstained face and discovered her brother standing at the entrance to the stall leaning on his crutches. Three weeks had wrought changes in him. He seemed older all of a sudden, more relaxed, and he sported a dark tan, evidence of the hours spent under a hot sun. She hadn't realized how much she missed him until now.

"Troy! I didn't know you were coming. You should have told me!" She hurriedly wiped her eyes and rushed over to give him a hug, but he held her at arm's length.

"I called the house before flying in with Randy, but you'd already left. One of the guys from the hangar dropped me off here. How come you're crying?"

"Because I'm so happy to see you." She flashed him a brilliant smile.

He frowned. "Alex, I've been standing here for ten minutes listening to you pour your heart out to that horse. Something's wrong. What is it?"

"Nothing earthshaking," she lied. "Come and meet Snow White."

"In a minute. First of all I have something important to tell you." He sounded dead serious, and it stopped her cold.

"Is it Zack? Has something happened to him?" she cried in alarm, her heart beating too fast.

"No," Troy answered in a quiet voice. "It's his father. He died night before last. Zack acts okay on the surface, but I can tell he's broken up. He loved his father the way we loved Mom and Dad." Troy's voice quavered.

Alex gave a slight gasp, then slid an arm around his waist. "I didn't know."

"According to Mac, who drove me here, it's been on TV and in all the newspapers."

Alex heaved a sigh. "I've been so busy with work and Snow White, I haven't watched TV, let alone found time to read the paper."

"You're not the only one. I didn't hear about it until a couple of hours ago, when Randy and I came back from a two-day roundup with Jocco. Randy flew in to meet his father's plane. There's going to be a memorial service at the ranch house in the morning, and then people will be coming by in the afternoon to pay their respects."

Alex imagined it would be an enormous crowd, but all she could really think about was Zack and the loss he must be feeling.

"I came home to tell you and to get my suit. I was hoping you'd drive me to the Circle Q early in the morning, in time for the service. Zack asked me to be a sort of honorary pallbearer."

"Are you serious?" It stunned Alex to realize Troy and Zack had become that close in so short a time.

"Yeah. Randy, too. Isn't that incredible—Zack asking me even though I'm still on crutches? You don't know how much it means to me. At nights I've been going in to help Randy read to his grandpa. Zack is always in there rubbing his back or brushing his hair. We've all gotten real close. The other night I was talking to Randy's grandpa and he blinked at me. I figured it was his way of saying he knew I was there. It was neat. Anyway, do you think we could send some flowers? I'll pay for them out of my salary."

"O-of course we'll send flowers, and forget about the money."

"Look, Alex. I know Zack said some cruel things to you, but he had good reason. There's some stuff in his past Randy's only hinted at, but I guess it's pretty much turned him off women. Randy says Zack will never get married because of it."

Troy could have no idea how his words affected her. She felt as if she'd just been shot through the heart at close range.

"And I found out things about Randy that would make your hair curl," Troy went on. "Zack made a promise to Randy's dad that he wouldn't let him get into any trouble while he was gone on his trip. When he thought you were the person manipulating our stupid mail-order business, he went kind of crazy."

"He went a lot further than that, Troy," she broke in. "He was ready to put both of us behind bars. Did he ever explain why he didn't just come to the house with the evidence and confront us like any normal person would have?"

"No. He keeps a lot of things to himself."

"Well, how lucky for him that he doesn't have to function in this world like the rest of us," she muttered.

"Alex, please don't be so upset. He's tried to make it up to you. Randy told me this little filly was his pride and joy. You don't still hate him, do you?"

"I-it doesn't really matter what I think, does it?" Alex averted her eyes and moved away from her brother, confused and troubled by each new revelation.

"Yeah, I think it does," Troy persisted. "Zack's been terrific to me," he said with another tremor in his voice. "He's easy to talk to, like Dad used to be. He never puts me down or tells me how to think. I know this is going to sound crazy to you, but I love the guy. He's the greatest."

Alex didn't have any trouble understanding that, because she'd been feeling the same thing—no, suffering from the same affliction—much longer than Troy. And there wasn't anything she could do about it, according to Troy, who'd been told that Zack would never marry. That was information only someone like Randy would be privy to.

Taking a deep breath, Alex squared her shoulders and said, "Let's go home. I have some arrangements to make if we're going to leave first thing in the morning."

"Thanks." Troy reached out and trapped her in a bear hug. "Thanks for coming. It means a lot to me."

When he let her go she gave Snow White another pat and whispered a promise to see her tomorrow night. Then she and Troy left for home.

On the way, Alex plied Troy with dozens of questions about everything he'd been doing, and she was treated to a fascinating account of ranch life that filled her with envy.

He was still going strong when they drove through the gates of the Circle Q the next morning. She was forced to park a good distance from the ranch house because of the long line of cars bordering the drive.

Since Alex hadn't had time to do any shopping, she hoped her simple black cotton dress, which buttoned up the front and flared softly at her knees, would be appropriate. She wore her mother's single strand of pearls and the matching pearl clip to hold her hair in place, pulled back from her forehead.

The last time Zack had seen her, she'd been a complete mess after a hard day's work and had no chance to freshen up. Of course, it was foolish to think he'd even notice her; this was his father's funeral, after all. Nevertheless, she wanted to look her best, out of respect for his sorrow and, she acknowledged simply, out of love.

Troy walked up the drive with her, carrying the spray of white roses they'd bought in Carson City. No florist shop in Reno would have been open so early, and neither she nor Troy wanted the flowers to arrive late.

The hearse stood parked in front. According to Troy, after the funeral the body would be driven to the family cemetery five miles away, where Zack's father would be buried next to his wife. Apparently she'd died soon after Zack was born of the same ailment that had brought about the recent death of Randy's mother.

The more Alex learned about Zackery Quinn, the more she realized he'd been through a lot of suffering in his life. To some extent this accounted for the darker side of his nature, and it made her reflect with more insight on their stormy relationship.

While Troy excused himself to deliver the flowers and take his place with Randy near the casket, Alex followed the line of people through the foyer to the living room. Chairs had been arranged in rows for the service. Many of the people were ranch hands and their families. Flowers overflowed the immense interior and someone was playing a hymn on the grand piano at the other end.

Her eyes automatically sought out the owner of the Circle Q and she identified him immediately. Dressed in a formal midnight-blue suit and tie, his hair cut shorter than she remembered, he looked astonishingly handsome. She could stare hour upon hour and never tire of looking at him.

He stood next to the closed casket, conversing with Governor Cordell, his brother-in-law, and the minister. As Troy approached on his crutches, she watched the warm way Zack greeted her brother, then accepted the flowers and put them on one of the stands nearby. She saw Troy whisper something to him, and Zack looked up with a start, scanning the faces in the crowd till his gaze came to rest on Alex.

Even from the distance separating them, his dark eyes seemed to pierce her, and she felt as if the breath was being squeezed from her lungs. While she stood on trembling legs, he took one white rose from the arrangement and, his eyes still on her, pressed it to his lips before placing it on top of the casket, beside a spray of red roses.

Her heart pounded so hard she thought she was going to pass out. She sat down abruptly in the first available seat. What did his gesture mean? What did she want it to mean?

Alex was only half-aware of the service, which proceeded along much the same lines as the one for her parents, with loving comments expressed by friends and colleagues. Eventually the minister made the closing remarks and a woman with a glorious operatic voice sang "God be with you till we meet again." But Alex could hardly concentrate, because of the swell of conflicting emotions inside her.

At last the service concluded and the pallbearers took their places. They included Zack, Andrew Cordell, Randy, Jocco, Pete and the dark attractive man Alex had seen in the small photos on Zack's mantel.

They slowly carried the casket out of the room to the waiting hearse. A solemn-looking Troy walked beside Randy. Alex noticed with pride how mature and dignified her brother looked. But she couldn't take her eyes off Zack as he passed, his expression one of deep reflection. The white rose lay conspicuously among the red. In light of the things Troy had told her about Zack's past, she was more puzzled than ever.

As soon as she could no longer see him, she read the rest of the memorial program. Those going to the grave site would follow, while the rest of the mourners would move to the dining room and patio area, where refreshments awaited. Since Troy wouldn't be going home with her, Alex decided now was a good time to leave for Reno. No matter how much she'd secretly hoped to see Zack again, this day belonged to him and his family, and she had no wish to intrude.

Slipping the program into her purse, she stepped into the crowded foyer. She'd almost reached the entryway when she felt a firm hand take hold of her wrist. She'd know Zack's touch anywhere, and she slowly turned her head, wondering why he hadn't gone out to the car with the rest of his family. Everyone must be waiting.

Zack pulled her aside. "I don't have time to explain," he whispered. "Just be here when I get back. I'm asking for Randy's sake."

For Randy's sake?

She watched in a daze as he released her to take the porch steps two at a time and climb inside the limousine.

"Ms. Duncan?" Alex whirled around at the sound of Yolanda's voice. "Zack said you'd be staying over. The room you used before is at your disposal. If there's anything you need, you can let me know by picking up the phone and ringing the kitchen extension."

"Thank you."

Bewildered by this turn of events, Alex hurried up the stairs to the second floor, anxious to escape from the strangers thronging Zack's home. More than that, she needed to be alone.

For a foolish moment, she'd thought Zack had asked her to stay because . . . because he felt the same way she did. But the second he mentioned Randy's name, the elation she'd been feeling changed to despair. It didn't make any sense, since Zack was a confirmed bachelor, anyway, and the most he could offer would be an affair.

To cheapen her deepest feelings and emotions with a relationship other than marriage would be a betrayal of everything she believed in. What irony that what *he* believed was the very opposite. Zackery Quinn wasn't about to surrender all that freedom to make his lover his wife.

Flinging herself across the bed, she buried her face in her arms, desolate because he hadn't even asked her to be his lover. She would have turned him down, of course.

But to hear the words, to know he wanted her that much ...

CHAPTER TEN

"ALEX?"

Troy's voice jarred her awake and she sat up, glancing at her watch. Two hours had gone by.

"Come in." She slid off the bed to smooth out her dress, then started looking for the high heels she'd kicked off earlier. But she stopped in her tracks when the door opened and she saw Zack standing behind Troy. An instant stillness pervaded the room as she stared into his searching eyes.

"We have a favor to ask," he said solemnly.

"Yeah," Troy interjected. "It's about Randy. He's upset because his dad had to leave right after the burial service. It was an emergency. He might not get back for a couple of days."

Zack's hands slid to Troy's shoulders as naturally as if the two of them had been together for a lifetime. "I've grieved over my dad's hopeless condition a long time and feel nothing but relief now that he's gone to his rest. But Randy's taking it hard because he and Dad had a close relationship, and this has come too soon after Wendie's death."

"You know how it feels, Alex," Troy muttered.

Yes. She knew.

"Troy and I talked it over and agree that Randy needs a distraction. So we've decided to take a camping trip into the mountains for a couple of days. If you come with us, it'll make a big difference in easing Randy's guilt. He's afraid you'll never forgive him for the part he played in the mail-order business. He doesn't need *that* on top of his grief."

Troy leaned on his crutches. "He thinks you hate him. He's really messed up about that."

"I've never hated anyone in my life!"

Something flickered deep in Zack's eyes. "Can you take an unexpected vacation without inconveniencing your clients too much?"

"If you need to call people, I'll help," Troy offered.

Her brother's pleading expression was transparent. But the enigmatic man standing behind him held his secrets too close for scrutiny. Still, he'd just come from burying the father he loved. She suspected that even the great Zackery Quinn might need to get away for a while. Might need to relax from all the worries and responsibilities of caring for his incapacitated father over the last few years.

The lines of strain bracketing his mouth and the slight smudge of shadow beneath his eyes testified to the tension he'd been under. Yet despite all his worries and commitments, his compassion reached out to his unhappy nephew, and she admired him for that more than she could say.

Fingering the pearls at her throat, she asked, "How long do you plan to be gone?"

"Three days maximum," Zack supplied, his gaze intent on her face. "After that I have something vital to take care of. It'll require my complete attention for a month at least." His voice sounded faraway. Alex felt a strange ache in her heart; she feared the business of the ranch would consume all his time and she might not see him again after this...

Three days might be all she'd ever have of him. Three days in which she might get to know what kind of person he'd been before he'd become embittered. What would that be like? More than anything in the world she wanted to find out.

Troy looked anxious. "What do you say, Alex? I don't want to go without you. Neither of us has taken a vacation since Mom and Dad died. If anyone deserves it, you do." His voice shook with emotion.

Alex couldn't remain immune to Troy's entreaty. Besides, he was right; they hadn't had a carefree moment in three years. And she certainly didn't want Randy to think she held anything against him. The motherless boy was suffering enough.

"How can you go camping with that cast?"

Before Troy could say anything, Zack explained. "There's a fire-break road up on the mountain. It ends at a little lake teeming with fish and surrounded by pines. We'll set up our tents there and do whatever we feel like."

Whatever we feel like. If he only knew...

She lowered her eyes to hide a growing excitement. "I'll need to go back to Reno and call a few people first, then put a message on the machine," she said, thinking out loud.

"While you do that, I'll help you pack and close up the house," Troy exclaimed with such eagerness she wouldn't have dared disappoint him.

Zack said, "We'll take the plane. That'll give us enough time to return to the ranch tonight and get everything ready to leave first thing in the morning."

"What about Snow White?" It had only just occurred to her that the filly would be left unattended.

Zack removed his hands from Troy's shoulders and started to unfasten his tie. Alex's eyes followed the movements of his tanned hands, fascinated by everything about him. "I'll give Jack a call and tell him to watch her while we're gone. No doubt she'll miss you, but from what I hear, you've been spoiling her to the point she doesn't want anyone else to handle her. A dry spell will do her good, considering she'll be getting a new owner soon."

"Did Jack tell you that?" she said in alarm.

"No," was the quiet response. "As I recall, *you* told me you couldn't keep her." His head tilted to the side. "Have you had a change of heart?"

Unable to sustain either of their curious glances, she brushed an imaginary piece of lint from her dress. "I-I've been too busy to advertise yet."

"Then there's no problem," Zack answered smoothly. "As soon as I've changed, I'll meet you in front of the house and we'll get going."

"I'm going to tell Randy," Troy cried excitedly, and he bolted for the door as best he could with crutches.

Left alone with Zack, she felt vulnerable and tongue-tied. He hadn't moved, and his gaze swept over her with an intimacy that reminded her of other times. Times when they'd been alone together...

Her mouth went dry and she moistened her lips nervously. "I'm afraid Troy's the only one in the family with camping gear."

"I have everything you'll need. All we require is your presence. Three days and nights in the mountains, and Randy's spirits should be vastly improved. By then his dad will be back and—I hope—find more time for his son."

"A boy should have a father." Her voice cracked. "You've been wonderful to Troy. I suppose you realize that he's really attached himself to you."

"I'm not complaining," he said in a low voice. "Over the past few weeks I've grown attached to your brother, too. He's a young man to be proud of. I'd like to have met your parents. They did a remarkable job of raising their children." Alex felt the heat pour into her cheeks. "Andrew could have used some of their wisdom."

He gave a heavy sigh and slid the tie from around his shirt collar. "Thank you for agreeing to accompany us, especially since I know how reluctant you are to come anywhere near me."

At that remark she looked up, surprising a bleak look that emphasized the severity of his features. "You had every right to slap my face and more," he went on. "I was a little insane then. But I swear on my father's grave I won't knowingly do anything to hurt you again. The boys have become fast friends. I'd like us to be friends, too. Do you think that's possible?"

No! Not when I'm dying with love for you.

How would she manage for three days and nights in his presence—eating, talking, sleeping around the camp fire, without giving away her deepest feelings?

"Alex?" His demand sounded urgent, reminding her of the reason he'd asked her to come along on this camp-out in the first place.

In a dull voice she said, "For Randy's sake, I'll try."

She felt the tension between them before he gave her a curt nod, his expression remote and unapproachable as he strode from the room.

Alex sank onto the end of the bed in a stupor. She'd agreed to go on the camp-out, so why did her answer change him into that forbidding stranger again? She couldn't imagine them lasting one hour, let alone three days!

THE MINUTE TROY ENTERED his friend's bedroom, Randy shut the door and locked it. They grinned at each other like long-time accomplices.

Troy punched Randy in the shoulder. "She fell for it. Right?"

"Yeah!" Randy exclaimed, his eyes shining. "So did Uncle Zack. He didn't even blink when I told him Dad was taking off after the funeral and I couldn't handle it. I hinted how I wished I could just get away for a while with him and you, but I knew you'd never go without your sister."

Troy laughed. "Didn't your dad mind doing that for us?"

"Nope. I sat down with him early this morning and told him about all the trouble we caused. At first it blew him away. He shook his head—and then he started to laugh. I told him about how it all backfired on Uncle Zack and how crazy he is about your sister. How he gave her Snow White. And how his plan to go slow and easy with her is driving him nuts, not to mention everybody else on the ranch.

"I told him what Pete said to Jocco—that a certain redhead's tying the boss up in knots. And that all the hands are keeping out of Uncle Zack's way these days. When Dad heard that, he said he'd give anything to see Uncle Zack hog-tied for good. Then I told him what Uncle Zack said about me inheriting the ranch someday because he'd never have a son of his own. That's what pushed Dad over the edge. He said he'd do whatever it took to make things work out, and he checked into a hotel in Reno for the night."

"Your dad sounds like a great guy."

"He is. He told me how much he missed me on this trip, how sorry he's been about leaving me on my own so much and how he wants us to be real close, like Uncle Zack was with Grandpa."

"That's great," Troy murmured with a lump in his throat. "Take him up on it, Randy. You never know when he might not be around anymore."

Randy nodded. "Yeah. Anyway, the great news is, everything's going according to plan. And you know what else Dad said before he left? He told me he was positive we had Grandpa Quinn's blessing, since grandpa's been worried for years about Uncle Zack being a bachelor."

"Hey, if my sister ends up marrying your uncle, what does that make you and me?"

"I don't know, but it'll sure be easier for us to start up another business. Steve'll want in again."

"Yeah. He's cool. You know, I've been thinking about those bookmarks the romance-writer lady ordered? The ones where I had to take a picture of that tough-looking dude running the jackhammer?"

"Yeah?"

"Well, if my sister flipped over your uncle Zack, then that means most of the females in America would, too. She took a ton of film that day on the ranch, and almost every picture is of him. She blew up one of him on his horse and has it stuck to the lamp shade at the side of her bed. Do you catch my drift?"

"Yeah." Randy smiled. "Mom used to say he broke a heart every time he smiled. Hey, maybe we could work up some Western calendars to sell to women who own horses. I know someone high up in the Arabian Horse Registry who'd be able to get us mailing lists."

"That's a great idea! And we won't have to use ham radio anymore. Everything legal this time."

"Let's talk about it after we get to Hidden Lake." They eyed each other meaningfully. "I'd say we're ready to put the rest of our plan into action."

"You know it. Now I better get downstairs. Alex will be waiting. By tomorrow night we should be well on our way to becoming officially related."

"Yeah."

AT SEVEN THE NEXT MORNING, after Alex had spent a restless night under Zack's roof fantasizing about being his wife and sleeping in his bed, she and Troy finished their breakfast and joined Zack and Randy out in front of the house. They'd been up early packing and were ready to go.

The minute Zack saw her coming down the steps, his dark eyes swept over her figure, clad in cotton shirt and Levis, sending a feverish warmth through her body. Her legs felt as insubstantial as jelly.

"Uncle Zack, how about if I ride in the back seat with Alex? There's more leg room for Troy's cast if he sits in front with you."

The fact that her first name came so easily to Randy's lips, in addition to his suggestion that they sit together, seemed to surprise Zack as much as it relieved Alex. Obviously Randy was becoming comfortable with her. Besides, there'd be less tension if there was a little distance between her and Zack. He was far too attractive in his white T-shirt and tight faded jeans for her peace of mind.

After a quiet pause he said, "That's a good idea, Randy," then came around the front of the car to open the passenger door. But Randy got there first. "After you, Alex."

"Thanks, Randy." She climbed inside and fastened her seat belt while everyone else clambered in. Zack shut his door with unnecessary vigor. A moment later they were off.

"I'm sure glad you agreed to come with us, Alex," Randy said once they'd passed through the main gate. "All along I've been thinking you hated me for what we did. The thing is, you really are beautiful. All my friends freaked out when they saw your picture."

Randy had irresistible charm when he chose to use it, just like his uncle Zack, Alex thought. She couldn't prevent the little smile that lifted the corners of her mouth. "Well, I have to admit I was furious at first. But now I've had time to think things over, and in a way, I'm kind of flattered. Any woman would be."

He grinned. "Hey, Troy? Did you hear that?"

Her brother turned in the seat so he could look at them. "I told you Alex wouldn't stay mad for long."

Randy stared at her. "That's good, because my dad wants to meet you."

At that remark she felt Zack's burning gaze through the rearview mirror. Afraid to acknowledge it, she said to Randy, "I'd like to meet him, too. He looks younger in person than he does on TV. He reminds me a little of Robert Redford in his younger days."

Suddenly the Rover seemed to accelerate.

"Yeah?" His eyes brightened. "Well, he thinks you're something else. I hope you won't be mad, but yesterday morning when I confessed everything to him, he asked to see some of your posters. And he freaked out, just like my friends! He said he could easily understand how we made so much money so fast."

"I thought I told you guys to get rid of everything," Zack ground out while Alex sat there horrified at the thought of Governor Cordell's seeing the photos.

"We did, but I kept a couple for souvenirs. Dad took my favorite. The one of you washing the car. He asked me to invite you to dinner as soon as we get back from camping."

"You're kidding!" She let out a nervous laugh.

"No." He shook his head and his expression grew more serious. "At first I thought he was teasing. You know, he hasn't looked at another woman since Mom died. He said that's because he hasn't been interested. Besides, he said he was afraid to ask anyone out in case it hurt me."

Alex bowed her head. "I can understand that."

"Yeah, well, he knows I don't have a problem where you're concerned, and he really does want to get to know you. He asked me a ton of questions, but he mainly wanted to know if you were interested in any other man. I told him you hadn't dated since you moved from California, and that made him really happy."

Either the mountain road had become a treacherous cow path, or Zack was driving too fast. If Alex hadn't been wearing her seat belt, she would have been hurled into Randy's lap.

"Hey, Alex," Troy said, "wouldn't it be cool if you and Randy's dad got together?"

"For heaven's sake, Troy!" she said, shocked by the entire conversation and extremely uncomfortable with the discussion in Zack's hearing.

"What's the harm in talking about it? You can't say it's impossible, can she, Zack." Troy turned to the man beside him. "I'd have a governor for a stepfather, and Randy and I would be brothers."

"Yeah," Randy chimed in. "And if you two had a baby, you'd have built-in sitters—Troy and me. You could go on fabulous trips with Dad and not have to worry about a thing."

"Think, Alex! You could end up Nevada's next first lady!"

"And it'd be all due to Uncle Zack." Randy leaned forward and put his hands on his uncle's broad shoulders. "At first I was mad that you found out about everything, but not anymore. Man, it would blow my friend's minds if Alex became my stepmom!"

"Aren't you boys getting a little ahead of yourselves?" Zack muttered in a voice Alex hardly recognized.

"I don't know, Uncle Zack. They have a lot in common. Dad loves to ride when we visit the ranch. Alex could keep Snow White there along with his horse. It would be perfect."

"I think you boys have been doing too much thinking. Give it a rest. For one thing, you're embarrassing Alex. It's time to change the subject." Zack's chill tone cut the conversation short.

"Okay." Randy sat back and Troy faced the front again. In a few more minutes Randy leaned across the seat and whispered to Alex, "Will you come to dinner with Dad? Please?"

There was an earnestness in his eyes and voice that reached a vulnerable spot in Alex, and she found herself nodding.

"I said that will be enough, Randy!"

"Jeez, Uncle Zack. I was just doing what Dad asked me to do. What's the big deal? I heard you tell him before he left on this last trip that you hoped he'd start living again. Didn't you mean it?"

By now Zack's growing anger made Alex want to get out of the Rover and run in the opposite direction. If only Randy would stop. He probably didn't realize all this talk of his father's remarrying hurt Zack, because emotionally he wasn't as ready as Randy to see Wendie Cordell supplanted in his brother-in-law's affections. And certainly not by Alex.

A new pain stabbed her. Apparently Zack didn't mind a little lovemaking with her on the side when he felt like it, but marriage to him or his brother-in-law was out of the question.

"Look, Uncle Zack," Randy explained, apparently heedless of the tension building in the car, "you've told me how you feel about marriage. Even Grandpa said you were hopeless in that department. Jeez, everyone knows *you* don't need a woman to be happy. But Dad's not like that. He loved Mom and I think he's ready to start loving someone again. As far as I'm concerned, Alex would be perfect. That's all I'm saying." His voice cracked with emotion and tears moistened his eyes.

The car came to a halt. With the engine still running, Zack put his hand on the back of the seat and turned to Randy, his expression grim. "Maybe this trip isn't such a good idea, after all. I meant what I said. If you can't find another topic of discussion, we'll go home. It's up to you."

Alex felt a jolt of alarm. Though the conversation had become far too personal, she thought Zack was being unnecessarily harsh on his nephew, whose emotions lay so close to the surface. Then she remembered that Zack had buried his father as recently as yesterday; he had his own raw feelings to contend with.

To her great relief, Randy didn't say another word. Troy remained uncharacteristically quiet, which meant he, too, must be aware of the tension, and they completed the drive to Hidden Lake in awkward silence.

Alex had never been so happy to get to a destination. The pine-rimmed lake, surrounded by mountains, was perfect in its beauty, but she hardly noticed. The minute they arrived, she jumped from the car and volunteered to unpack their lunch while the others made camp.

The boys steered clear of Zack and set up their tent beneath a huge pine, while he pitched two other tents a short distance away to ensure privacy. Every so often she felt his glance on her, watching her movements. She tried to behave as if she wasn't aware of it, but inwardly she felt nervous and jittery. It was the same way she felt when a huge storm was about to blow in.

Putting the portable camp table in place, Alex set out the fried chicken and potato salad and announced lunch. Zack followed the boys, who were deep in conversation, his expression as dark as a thundercloud.

"Hey, Alex?" Randy addressed her as she passed him a root beer from the cooler. "Troy wants to take a nap after lunch, so why don't you come fishing with me and I'll show you Dad's favorite spot. It's around the other side of the lake. There's this little pocket formed by rocks and he always catches trout there. He'd kill me if I gave away his secret to anyone else, but he won't mind if—"

Zack cut him off coldly. "Alex is going on a hike with me, Randy. Now I suggest you eat your lunch, and then it'll be your turn to clean up. We probably won't be back until dinner."

"I'll cook it, Randy," Troy offered cheerfully. "You catch the fish and I'll fry them. Alex taught me how to fix trout this special way, didn't you, Alex?" He looked to her for affirmation, then turned back to Randy and said in an aside, "She's a fabulous cook. So was my mom. Dad said that was one of the reasons he married her. Your dad will love Alex's trout, if you catch my drift. Too bad he's not here." Then he managed to consume a whole deviled egg in one bite.

"Yeah," Randy answered before draining his root beer. "But there's always next time. Dad's birthday is in three weeks. We always come up here. I wouldn't be surprised if he invites Alex along." He smiled at Alex as he said it.

"If you're ready, let's go," Zack said in an arctic voice.

Leaving part of his food untouched, he got up from the log he'd been sitting on. Even if Alex hadn't wanted to go hiking, she would never have said otherwise, not when he looked so...so forbidding.

Alex followed his long strides as they made their way to the other side of the lake. They started climbing a ridge, the summit of which Zack said, would give them a spectacular view.

Normally she would have marveled at the grandeur of this untouched unspoiled place and would have stopped to take pictures of everything. But with Zack in this black frame of mind, she couldn't concentrate on anything.

The intense heat made her thirsty, and when they came to a little brook beneath the trees, they decided to stop for a drink. Alex knelt on the grassy bank and held her braid while she immersed her face in the cool water. When she lifted her head, she discovered Zack crouched down, watching her.

"You're angry," she murmured. "Why? What horrible crime have I committed now? I thought you wanted me to come—for Randy's sake."

His features hardened. "Randy has always been a complicated boy, and he's not himself right now. I'm sorry if his fantasies about you and Andrew have embarrassed you. I apologize for that."

She blinked. "I'm not embarrassed. In fact I'm rather touched."

Her response didn't appear to please him. If anything, the frown lines on his face deepened. "Nevertheless, any kind of relationship he imagines you having with Andrew is out of the question."

Alex was suddenly furious. "Aside from the fact that if I want to accept a dinner invitation from your brother-in-law it's absolutely none of your business, might I ask why you're warning me off?" She tried to control the anger in her voice but failed. "Is it because I don't come from a monied background like your sister, therefore I'm unacceptable? Or is it because you want Andrew to be as miserable as you are, and you can't bear to see anyone else take your sister's place in his affections? Randy wasn't so far off the mark, was he?"

She jumped to her feet, her heart beating triple time. By now Zack had joined her, his hands clenched into fists, but she was beyond caring.

"You didn't mean it when you told Andrew to start living again," she lashed out. "Your perceptive nephew certainly has you figured out. Your soul is so scarred you'd drag everyone else down with you! Well, thank heavens your bitterness hasn't rubbed off on Randy. He's an honest, normal young man who wants a happy family life. He's entitled to it, you know. And I'm going to accept that dinner invitation." Her heart rejoiced when she saw the blood drain from his face.

"Your brother-in-law happens to be a very attractive man. And if he found my photograph appealing, then what's wrong with that? What better way for two people to start off a relationship than knowing there's a physical attraction? And if we should fall in love and get married," she went on, suspecting that her face was as red as her hair, "there won't be anything *you* can do about it."

She squared her shoulders, preparing to march back to the campsite. "You might be master of all you survey, Mr. Zackery Quinn, but you won't be giving orders beyond the boundaries of the Circle Q. You and your ranch deserve each other. Enjoy your loneliness!"

Too furious to spit out another word, she started to bolt, but his arm shot out and grabbed her leg. She ended up facedown on the grassy bank.

"Oh!" she cried, more from surprise than hurt. Still fighting to catch her breath, she couldn't say a word. That was when she felt his hard body slide against hers. When she tried to roll over, she couldn't, because he'd pinned her arms above her head.

"It's this red hair of yours," he whispered in a husky voice as he proceeded to unfasten her braid, "You were in such a temper I didn't think I was ever going to get a word in." Alex gasped as he kissed the nape of her neck exposed by the collar of her blouse. "Now that I've got you almost where I want you, you're going to listen to me." He bit her earlobe gently, igniting the flame that flared every time he touched her.

"Don't you know the only reason I can't abide the thought of you anywhere near Andrew or Ron or any other man is that I want you for myself?" He pressed hot kisses to her cheek and the corner of her mouth, driving her crazy with desire. She fought it and tried to hide her face in the grass.

"Well, I don't want you!" she finally managed.

"That's not what your body's telling me. Or your heart." His hands had started caressing her, and she moaned with need, unable to stop the traitorous response that compelled her to turn in his arms until she was gazing up at him, her hair spilling onto the grass.

A shadow crossed his face, clouding the glaze of passion in dark eyes. "You love me," he said in a voice thickened by emotion. "Say it, Alex. If you don't, then there's no purpose to my existence."

"And what about mine?" The question was pulled from her heart. "Do you have any idea what it's been like for me? Every word I've said you've twisted, every overture I've made you've repulsed. No one can stand that kind of anger and rejection."

"I know," he whispered, his eyes glittering with moisture. "But I'm begging you to listen to me."

Alex trembled from the pain and humility she saw in his face. "Troy mentioned something about a bad experience in your past..."

His jaw tensed. "It was more than a bad experience, Alex. It destroyed my belief in love, or so I thought until I was besotted by photographs of a certain luscious redhead. Dear Lord, Alex, I'm so in love with you it's tearing me apart. But I'm afraid..." His voice trailed off and she spied a glimpse of fear.

"*You?* Afraid?"

"You haven't heard my story."

"Then tell me," she said simply.

He grasped her hands and kissed them, his eyes haunted. "It's ugly. I risk losing you if I tell you."

"The only way you could ever lose me is if you stop loving me."

His eyes closed tightly for a moment. "I hope you mean that," he whispered against her lips, kissing her with an aching tenderness. "During my sophomore year in college, I met a dancer in one of those revues at Tahoe and I fell for her. Hard."

"You fell in love with a showgirl?" Alex conjured up an image of an exotically beautiful woman.

"That's right. Her name was Desirée. My buddies challenged me to go backstage and ask her for a date. When I hesitated, my oldest friend, Miguel, suggested I keep my identity a secret. That was so no one in my family would get any word of my activities. They would never have approved.

"Miguel always has good sense, so I acted on his advice and went to her dressing room, introducing myself with a fictitious name. To my amazement, she agreed to go out with me, and we started seeing each other on a regular basis."

He sighed and continued, "Needless to say, my studies went to hell that semester, because I spent every possible moment with her at her lavish apartment, which I thought her manager must have provided for all his dancers. When she told me I might as well move in with her, since we were sleeping together, anyway, I asked her to marry me, assuming of course that she wanted the same thing.

"In my naïveté, I imagined she'd jump at the chance. Naturally, I didn't want her taking off her clothes in front of anyone else, and I could hardly wait to tell her the truth about who I was. She'd come from an underprivileged home and I wanted to give her the world."

It was Alex's turn to close her eyes. She knew what was coming and hated to hear it.

"She laughed in my face and told me I was still a green kid, wet behind the ears, who had a lot to learn about women. She said she was never going to bring children into the world, not after being battered around with eight other kids by her alcoholic parents. She said a lot of things that shocked me at the time, things I won't bother to repeat, but in essence she killed whatever burgeoning interest I had in becoming a husband and father."

Zack sighed again. "Her rejection was a devastating blow. I dropped out of school and took off for

Europe with Miguel. We spent six months doing whatever we felt like. I went through one woman after another and even tried to fall in love with Miguel's distant cousin, a beautiful girl who lived in the Pyrenees.''

"Was she the woman in the picture on your mantel? The one standing between you and your friend?''

"No. That was Marieli, Miguel's wife,'' he murmured, wrapping a curl around his finger. "One day I'll tell you all about him and his disaster of a marriage. Anyway, at some point I came to my senses and decided it was time to go home and get on with my life.

"I went back to school, but to my shame, I still couldn't stop thinking about Desirée. That is, until Andrew, who by then was married to Wendie and already involved in politics, took me aside and told me something that burned out every bit of feeling that might of remained for her.''

"What?'' Alex urged when he didn't say anything more.

He took a long shuddering breath. "For one thing, he found out through Bud Atkins, a private investigator, that her real name was Jill Clifford. For another, he had proof that she was making pornographic movies on the side. That was, of course, what paid for that expensive apartment.''

Alex cringed and clutched him tighter.

"The news sickened me, revolted me. I couldn't believe I'd fallen for a woman who could do that. I decided there must be something warped in my nature if I wanted a woman like that. If I couldn't even see through her.''

"Oh Zack." The pieces of the puzzle were falling into place.

"There's more, Alex," he said quietly. "Someone tipped her off that I was a Quinn. While I was in Europe, she went to my father and tried to blackmail him by threatening to expose our affair to the media. She thought my father would cave in to her demands to prevent his reputation from being ruined. She had the audacity to ask for a million dollars."

"I hope he laughed in her face!" Alex burst out savagely. "What a fool she was! She could have had *you*. You're more priceless than all the money on earth!"

Zack crushed her to him and didn't speak for a long time. At last he said, "Dad reminded her that she could have been a millionaire many times over if she'd accepted my marriage proposal. But since she'd declined, she didn't have a leg to stand on. Furthermore, he warned her that if she tried to do anything to sully the Quinn name, he'd press charges. My father can be a formidable adversary, and she left the state the next day."

"Your father sounds like quite a man."

"He was, Alex. He was a good man, maybe a great one. You know, if Andrew hadn't told me about her blackmailing scheme, Dad would never have said a word. He loved me without qualification and never once threw my past mistakes or poor judgment back in my face."

"I wish I could have met him."

"So do I, sweetheart."

Then the reality of what he'd told her sank in, and she leaned back to look at him. "No wonder you treated me the way you did," she said slowly. "You must have thought I was Jill all over again, out to exploit your nephew and blackmail Andrew. The parallel is incredible. Now I understand why you've been so suspicious of me and so anxious to protect your family. I love you all the more for doing everything in your power to keep them from getting hurt.

"The fact is, you're a very loving man, and it was unfortunate that you happened to give your heart to the wrong person. But it happens to a lot of people. She was the loser, darling. I feel sorry for her—and so happy for me."

Zack shook his head, his eyes still full of torment. "How can you say that after everything I've told you? I'm not proud of my past, Alex, and after the hateful way I've treated you, I don't have the right to ask you to marry me."

"Don't put me on a pedestal, Zack. I'm far from perfect—something you're going to find out after we're married!"

"I already know all your secrets," he confessed in a low voice. "As Bud said, you're so squeaky clean someone ought to erect a monument to you."

Her eyes widened. "You had me investigated?"

He sucked in a breath. "I know more about you than you probably know about yourself."

"You're joking! Aren't you?" When he didn't say anything, she started to laugh. She didn't stop until she saw the serious look on his face. Then her laughter subsided.

"It's not funny, Alex. I even went so far as to have your photographs circulated to all the club and revue owners around the Tahoe area to discover if you worked there nights."

"Listen to me, darling. After what you've told me, I don't blame you for doing whatever you could to protect Randy. The only crime you're guilty of is not forgiving yourself. I love you, Zackery Quinn. All of you, every wonderful part.

"If you don't think you have the right to ask me, then I'll ask you. Will you marry me? Will you be my husband? Will you be the father of my children?" Her voice choked with emotion.

"Alex, oh, yes. Yes!" He rolled onto his back, taking her with him, then kissed her in mindless ecstasy. After long moments he pulled back and looked into her face. "Will you marry me tonight, as soon as I can get us back to the ranch?"

"Do you even have to ask?"

"Jeez, Uncle Zack! It took you long enough to pop the question!" Randy leapt out from behind a tree, startling them both. "I thought you'd never ask her. Now that she's said she'll marry you, can we leave? It'll only take a few minutes to pack the Rover. Troy wants to get back to work and I want to go home. Dad's waiting for me."

Alex's heart was too full to be angry at Randy and Troy for manipulating them into the outing or intruding on such a private moment. And the look of joy on Zack's face told her he didn't care if the whole world saw their passionate embrace. Everything she ever wanted to see was there in his eyes. Love. Love for her.

"Dad said you two would need a chaperon, and he wasn't kidding. He told me to watch you like a hawk. That's one for the books." She could hear Randy's happy laughter all the way down the ridge as he shouted the good news to Troy.

"Somehow I forgive them for everything, because they brought us together," Zack whispered against her lips. "My problem now is how to keep my hands off you until we get back to the ranch." After another prolonged kiss he said, "If you ever stopped loving me, my world would end. You know that, don't you?"

"Zack," she whispered back, but she was too full of emotion to express her love with words. All she could do was show him. As she would show him in the years ahead....

* * * * *

What about Andrew Cordell—will he discover happiness and new love? Find out in Rebecca Winters's next Romance, coming in 1994.

Calloway Corners

In September, Harlequin is proud to bring readers four
involving, romantic stories about the Calloway sisters,
set in Calloway Corners, Louisiana. Written by four of
Harlequin's most popular and award-winning authors,
you'll be enchanted by these sisters and the men
they love!

MARIAH by Sandra Canfield
JO by Tracy Hughes
TESS by Katherine Burton
EDEN by Penny Richards

As an added bonus, you can enter a sweepstakes contest
to win a trip to Calloway Corners, and meet all four
authors. Watch for details in all Calloway Corners books
in September.

CAL93

Harlequin Romance invites you...

BACK TO THE RANCH

As you enjoy your Harlequin Romance® BACK TO THE
RANCH stories each month, you can collect four proofs of
purchase to redeem for an attractive gold-toned charm bracelet
complete with five Western-themed charms. The bracelet will
make a unique addition to your jewelry collection or a
distinctive gift for that special someone.

One proof of purchase can be found in the back pages of each
BACK TO THE RANCH title...one every month until
May 1994.

To receive your gift, please fill out the information below and mail four (4) original proof-of-
purchase coupons from any Harlequin Romance **BACK TO THE RANCH** title plus $2.50 for
postage and handling (check or money order—do not send cash), payable to Harlequin Books,
to: **IN THE U.S.:** P.O. Box 9056, Buffalo, NY, 14269-9056; **IN CANADA:** P.O. Box 621, Fort
Erie, Ontario, L2A 5X3.

Requests must be received by June 30, 1994.

Please allow 4-6 weeks after receipt of order for delivery.

```
BACK TO THE       NAME: _____
                  ADDRESS: _____
  RANCH           _____
                  CITY: _____
                  STATE/PROVINCE: _____
                  ZIP/POSTAL CODE: _____
                  ACCOUNT NO.: _____

                  ONE PROOF OF PURCHASE        091 KAX
```